MAY WE BORROW YOUR COUNTRY

The Whole Kahani

Published by Linen Press, London 2019
8 Maltings Lodge
Corney Reach Way
London
W4 2TT
www.linen-press.com

A CIP catalogue record for this book is available from the British Library.

Cover art and design: Noruttam Dobey
Typeset by Zebedee Design, Edinburgh
Printed and bound by Lightning Source

ISBN 9781999604660

THE WHOLE KAHANI

The Whole Kahani (The Complete Story) is a collective of British novelists, poets and screenwriters of South Asian origin: Reshma Ruia, Kavita A. Jindal (co-founders), Mona Dash, Radhika Kapur, CG Menon, Shibani Lal, Deblina Chakrabarty and Nadia Kabir Barb. Between them, they have an array of awards and their first anthology *Love Across a Broken Map* was published in 2016 to critical acclaim.

www.thewholekahani.com.

Photograph by Jags Parbha

ACKNOWLEDGEMENTS

The Whole Kahani are grateful to Lynn Michell of Linen Press for championing this project with inspiration, charm and boundless patience. We would also like to thank Christopher Eggett for his help in editing some of the short stories and Jennifer Schwartz for selecting and editing all the poems.

CONTENTS

FOREWORD

Preti Taneja

There can never be a single story. There are only ways of seeing.[1]
— Arundhati Roy

Beyond the dangerous single story, there is the possibility of the whole story. It can never be written by one single writer. It can never hold characters from just one country, nor can it be policed according to the author's identity as stated in their passport. The whole story cannot only contain one language or one accent, one register or narrative voice or genre, gender, age, body type or set of social experiences. It must contain multitudes.

This is what I take from Roy's powerful assertion made in her 2002 lecture 'Come September' as a critique of Western media narratives after the September 11 attacks, and from Chimamanda Ngozi Adichie in her 2009 essay, 'The Danger of a Single Story.'[2]

---

1 Roy, Arundhati, 'Come September' in *The Ordinary Person's Guide to Empire*, A. Roy, (London: Flamingo 2014) p.14. Roy's statement was inspired by the work of writer and visual artist John Berger.

2 Adichie, Chimamanda Ngozi, *The Danger of a Single Story*, TED Global, (2009) https://www.ted.com/talks/chimamanda_adichie_the_danger_of_a_single_story [accessed 11 November, 2018]

The two writers break down the damage a dominant culture causes to people's perceptions when it relentlessly uses narrative to turn those of a different race, religion, ethnicity or gender into alien 'others.' It begins with the slow death of empathy, leaving groups of people ever more divided from each other, able to judge each other only by the stereotypes they have been sold. The devastations that follow feed war, terrorism, street level and domestic violence; they promote the patronising pity of a person from a wealthy nation towards the generic 'peoples' of a less advantaged one. Hierarchies of power are strengthened. Brutal structural prejudice remains intact. In many countries this means that generations of minority communities, and women from those communities in particular, are prohibited from accessing our rights, including to participate and benefit from cultural life: not only as consumers but also and more vitally, as makers.

As a direct result of the British Empire and the subsequent division of the Indian subcontinent in 1947 and '71, people of Indian, Pakistani and Bangladesh origin make up the majority of Britain's largest ethnic minority group, South Asians. Yet it is a truth, (if not one universally acknowledged) that novels and collections of short stories and poetry by British Asian people, particularly women, and even more significantly, by middle and working class women of South Asian origin are not found in numbers on the lists of the nation's main publishers, or adequately represented as characters in fiction. Do we not write? We do. Do we write ghost stories, crime fiction and modernist novels, historical fiction and erotica, politically charged epics, YA and children's books? Poetry, lyrical or formal and with its roots in myriad traditions? We do. And do we struggle to find representation? Then struggle to find editors who 'love' and 'get' the myriad styles of our work? From writer after writer I have heard from, (and in my own experience,) we do.

I wonder why this is, and I think about the single story of women from the Indian subcontinent – that we are docile, servile, perfect daughters, sisters, brides and mothers: sensual but not sexual, good for nothing but to be handmaids to patriarchy by making sons; proud to service a strict social order in which our place is predicated by factors including caste and religion, class and gender and happy to sacrifice our voices for a masculine, heroic narrative of nationhood. It will come as no surprise that to me, King Lear's final, hugely influential verdict on his youngest daughter Cordelia (which goes against almost everything we actually see of her in the play) might have been written as an epitaph for this woman: 'Her voice/ was ever soft, Gentle and low, an excellent thing in woman.' It is a single story that suits the tellers (brown and white,) because it protects their privilege.

I think about how few of the stories I read by women of South Asian origin actually feature such a female, and yet how this myth persists, and what damage it continues to do. I think about all the young, brown-girl readers, sitting behind a curtain in a window seat on a rainy day, dreaming of becoming writers and of making a place for themselves in our cultural life. They might even hope to leave a recognized body of work behind them. They might dream of being read on their own terms.

Imagine one of them. If she is British Asian she will first have to negotiate the push and pull of love and duty that various layers of South Asian patriarchy, class, race, religion or caste in her particular family ask of her, and then her voice in her locale, and simultaneously in the majority white world. It's a difficult way to live, especially when both mainstream British and Asian cultures are equally happy to read her body as passive, her mind and tongue agreeably silent, and further, to collude in a cultural system that maintains the status quo. From the UK to Australia, Sweden to Singapore her struggle might be a variation on this theme, with its own local contentions as the wise, witty and warm stories in this book show.

Reading it, it becomes clear that the UK cannot, as a participant player in global cultural production, nor as a country in the grip of an insular, fraught, soul-searching moment into what our national story is, arrive at a complete understanding of ourselves until the voices of British women of colour are equally heard. An easy thing to call for: a difficult thing to wait for. To hope for. Women can (apparently) keep doing that, endlessly. Or, we can organise across race and class, age, educational opportunity and career stage, to write and collect and publish words together. We can take Roy's and Adichie's assertions and make them visible.

May We Borrow Your Country is published by Linen Press: the only independent women's press in the UK. The term, 'independent women' has deeper resonance for these writers, when the overlapping patriarchal traditions of the home and the world are taken into account. Linen Press publishes work by women of all backgrounds, and by definition promotes women's solidarity as well as our psychological and social emancipation. In 2018, it is still on these various margins that such work is being made.

The writers are from the self-organising collective The Whole Kahani, they are critically acclaimed and new British writers of South Asian origin. It is the second anthology the group has published and it includes some quiet triumphs; the pieces are reflective and self reflective, humorous and surreal. They engage ingeniously with our digital future, they movingly explore the lasting impact of politically motivated violence; they take risks to bring alive the nuances of our various linguistic and cultural worlds.

So: women write. Around our adventures in love, our care for sick parents and small children, around going to school and to other work of all kinds, writing is being done. The fact of this important book, its authors, and contents and its production, not only highlight the mainstream's lack, it shows the power of a collective in the political sense: one formed with the understanding that it is not only finding space to do one's own work that matters, but also to organise, meet, communicate, support and encourage – in the sense of have faith in, or lend courage to – each other to write in the first place, and to keep writing, and to seek publication together; to edit, and to proof read and market and all of the other tasks which have here been shared – many of them on volunteered time.

Just as the whole story must include writers who are women, it follows that it must also include many female characters, exploring their complex emotions, their desires. What for? Everything, these writers wonderfully suggest. Time alone, sex. New clothes for self-expression; support from the men in their families, communities and work places. Though the list seems quite general, the specificities of culture are drawn here from across the globe. In the clever, funny SMALL FISH by Deblina Chakrabarty, a bright young woman new to Delhi's political class wryly observes that the 'country where elections were fought on vegetarianism was teeming with carnivores in denial.' Eventually she finds a fishy way to resist patriarchy's much-peddled drug of choice: self-loathing. In Radhika Kapur's brilliantly subversive THE METALLIC MINISKIRT, Divya, newly married, arrives in England full of romantic dreams culled from Western movies. With tender precision, Kapur shows how she struggles under her mother-in-law's strict gaze, only finding privacy after a long bus ride to the 'big Tesco.' Later, she escapes: wearing nothing but a metallic miniskirt in the shower, she becomes the centre of her own story, subverting the tired Bollywood 'wet sari' sequence that is usually performed with a lover. We, the silent readers are her only audience as she lifts her legs and the water rains down.

The pieces here also wrestle with the usual questions all writers face. How to create characters of another faith, age, gender, class or caste in a believable and ethical way? Is punctuation negotiable for purpose, should non-English terms be italicised, should they be translated in the text or must there be a glossary? What about accents? How can the rhyming pairs that might characterise the colloquial aspect of a language – in this case, Hinglish – be presented without falling into parody, or making its speakers and the language itself seem no more than bastard brown cousins to the English?

Nadia Kabir Barb's lovely, elegiac story LIVING WITH THE DEAD explores the differences in how Islam and Christianity deal with bodies, and with death rituals. When Bina, a Muslim says, 'I don't think London is a ditch-rich area,' Barb elegantly has both words of the phrase mean what they imply, instead of simply having them rhyme for rhyme's sake. London, Bina means, does not contain many ditches. In contrast, Shibani Lal's A LAUGHING MATTER has the narrator, Gaurav, returning after years spent in London to his home city 'Bombay', discovering

16

that he doesn't quite belong. While he wants to avoid 'expatness' and feels free to make up this word, he now hears the working class characters' Indian English in sharp relief. By writing their voices in heightened phonetic style, Lal examines Gaurav's sense of place, both social and geographical with disturbing effect.

Another central question that these writers tackle is how to show the double helix of honour and shame that postcolonial subjects inherit as a bad strand of DNA. Reshma Ruia's complex, bittersweet story A SINGLE MAN gives us Pikku, an Indian immigrant working in a London museum, trying to commit an impossible crime. Ruia writes him falling prey to his postcolonial genes: his own racism against black people is the result of his privileged childhood in Idi Amin's Uganda, and is offset by the racism he experiences from a white colleague at work. He still feels the childhood pain of being a boy less smart than his sister; he is also programmed to receive her admiration by dint of his sex. When an Indian artist shows in the museum, the story becomes a study of how tokenism in the Western art world impacts on invisible immigrants. Pikku and his sister's longing for 'home' morphs into pride in the Indian stranger's success. It is a way of sharing, however vicariously, in any recognition that someone with the same race or ethnicity achieves: it makes them feel (however fleetingly or wrongly,) seen. Pikku's sudden, surreal turn to crime is triggered by the fact that people of colour who 'make it' as artists at that level are few and far between.

Any collection of work by very different writers, and about people from various backgrounds requires its readers to be attentive to its tonal shifts. When one character wants to tell another 'every single detail in detail,' of a photograph we experience her delight in experimenting with a newfound language, just as we enjoy the description, later on in the piece that she is going 'mental, crack and fully mad.' And the uneasy sympathy we feel for Kumar, the grieving father in CG Menon's powerfully unheimlich story FOX CUB is underlined by Kumar's own, delicately drawn sense of the strangeness of his world, rooted in his outsider instinct that the country he lives in is not, will never be 'home.' As Menon brilliantly observes, it will always be a place in which snow is 'unsettling', and in which the existence of beggars is shocking as it never was in India.

Finally, it is in poems by Kavita A. Jindal and Mona Dash that the full power of this collection is revealed. In the devastating LETTER FROM THE GLASSHOUSE OPERA Jindal thinks through ways of seeing: an unnamed writer relives the trauma of losing a loved one in a guerilla war, while she is caught in a bright prism of music by Schubert and Mozart. The sounds and voices unlock memories, variations on themes: the relationship of men's art to women, of west to east is one of appropriation, and so the lesson is learned. In exchange, our writer doesn't choose to make material from her losses; she just has to: 'Everything you say and don't say/ will make it to the page even when it kills me. / You are fodder/ and this is the straw I hold./ It is one way of looking at it,' and later, 'Nancy was fodder; Mozart wrote an aria./ That's one way of looking at it.' The poem is a subtle call for a more complete way of seeing; it cleverly leaves readers to take this task forwards.

Though Dash's IMPLICATIONS captures the myriad micro-aggressions that her unnamed female-writer faces from all sides, and makes for uncomfortable, on point reading, the poem's last line is full of hope. When Dash writes, 'finding intersectionality: implied: *a pinpoint*' she evokes butterfly species categorised and pinned behind glass. But she also offers the wild, exhilarating sense that a new country where intersectionality might be the norm without its constituent parts having to be defined, can be written and read into being, then pinpointed, as a tiny country can be marked on a map. May we borrow it? Maybe it already exists and we live in it, only now, with this vital, tender, thrilling work, we might understand it better.

Preti Taneja, November 2018.

THE METALLIC MINI SKIRT

Radhika Kapur

I was scraping the tomatoes and their beady juices from the chopping board into the pan of simmering bright, green *bhindi*, but my mind had already taken flight. I imagined hot water cascading down my neck and back. My finger smudging a wet path down steamy, beige tiles. The shower is my favourite room in the house. It's like watching *Kuch Kuch Hota Hai* on Star TV for the 27th time. It's where I find peace. At my side, my mother-in-law's flour-dusted hands rolled out rotis with practised ease. She looked my way sharply when I sighed, and turned off the gas. She plunged in a spoon and scooped up the *bhindi*, blew on it three times and sucked it clean. I waited.

'Don't put in so many tomatoes next time. It makes it too sour,' she said. I liked the water hot, the lever turned to the right. I envisaged it washing my skin. Troubles sliding down my shoulders, swirling and disappearing down the dotted drain cover. 'You will get your wife degree the day Sunny can't tell who has

21

cooked, you or me!' she boomed, raising the spoon in her hand victoriously.

'Yes mummy,' I murmured.

Chandigarh
One year earlier

'A proposal has come for me, from London,' I whispered to Sunita on the phone.

'Aoi!' She screamed for a whole minute. I could visualise her jumping up and down like those glossy heads of hair in shampoo ads. She then lowered her voice conspiratorially. 'Have you seen a photo? Do you like him?'

I nodded. 'He's kind of cute-shute,' I giggled.

Sunita and I met at the Titanic Mela so I could tell her every single detail in detail. We were, as the name suggests, inside a giant cardboard replica of the Titanic. In one corner stood cut-outs of Kate Winslet and Leonardo DiCaprio with Kate's hands outstretched and Caprio's hugging her waist. Next to it, a motor spurred the grand Ferris wheel into slow motion. I clutched the latch of our red and yellow swaying carriage while Sunita nudged me, eyes gleaming.

'Boys abroad are better lovers,' she said confidently.

'How do you know, you've never had one?' I asked.

'Don't you watch English movies?' she rolled her eyes.

I tittered, eyes sliding away, fiddling with the gossamer gold circle around my flushed neck. I looked down at a child jumping excitedly, pointing at the wheel. The ground was teeming with *chole-bhature* and *chaat* stalls, whirring pots of pink candyfloss, twirling merry-go-rounds and loud speakers hoisted on long wooden poles.

I met Sunny in the red plastic interior of Cafe Coffee Day two weeks later. He had come to India to meet his shortlist of girls.

Boys abroad are better lovers. Sunita's words echoed in my head as I gazed into his deep brown eyes, the colour of melted Dairy Milk. His lashes were long, his nose had a little bump in the middle. I imagined running my finger over that nose as we sipped our cappuccinos.

He went home that night and told his mother that he didn't want to meet any more girls. She sat bolt upright on the bed and flung down the newspaper she was reading. 'Thank you, God,' she screeched. She couldn't believe her duty as a mother was done so fast.

The next day I went with my parents to meet his mother. When I folded my hands in greeting, she crushed me in her cushiony embrace. My held breath unfurled as she let me go. It wasn't the only time she would choke me.

My parents were ecstatic.

Ma said, 'You already know how to speak in an accent,' referring to my call centre job where I was trained to deal with American customers. 'You'll get a good job very quickly.' A job in London? Oh my God, my head just spun at the thought.

London beckoned like paradise. It was out of India. I had never been out of India. Sunita said you get pre-cut vegetables in the supermarket there. Such a cool idea. Pre-cut vegetables. The first world is the first world, *bhai*! Even their vegetable shops are more advanced than ours. What would the rest of the country be like? I wanted to see Buckingham Palace, ride the red London buses and dance the night away in slick nightclubs. I daydreamed about the short skirt I would wear.

I took Sunny shopping to test whether he would object if I

23

bought one. I watched him from the corner of my eye as I slid my hand across the rack and picked out a shiny, metallic mini skirt. He raised an eyebrow, then, jauntily, his thumb. I hugged his startled frame. He didn't know he had just passed the exam. I stood, my hands on my hips, looking at my reflection in the mirror in the small changing room. The mini skirt hugged my hips. I pushed my lips into a pout, flicked my hair back and held my waist like models do. Ooh la la. The thing is that if you wear revealing clothes, people say you are fast and that no one will marry you. But, once I am married and I wear my skirt, what will they say? Ha! I'll outwit those old busybodies. The seven rounds of the holy fire that Sunny and I will walk on our wedding day will be my freedom.

The day after the wedding, I quickly changed my status on FB from Divya Sodhi to Divya Khanna. I stared at my new name onscreen and rolled it over my tongue: DIVYA KHANNA, DIVYA KHANNA, DIVYA KHANNA. It sounded like the horn that blares just before a train pulls away from the platform, when passengers still buying wafers, *kulhad* tea or water from the stalls run and jump into their compartments. My new name was a signal that a whole new life was about to pick up speed. I exhaled. Then the pinging sounds began. 103 likes by the end of the day!

The night before I left, I looked at my cupboard. Well actually, it was a fridge. Not a working one of course. It became my cupboard when it stopped working. Ma said that there was no need to throw out something useful. Doesn't every house have an object that is transformed into another? The t-shirt that becomes the duster or the tyre that becomes a swing. Sunita's house even has a broken washing machine that's used as a table.

Anyway, back to my cupboard. Ma always scolded me because it was so untidy, clothes dumped on top of each other, but now only a few old clothes remained in it. When I saw the aching emptiness, I broke into heaving sobs, head resting against its smooth whiteness. Then Sunita called. She was crying too.

'You were right, by the way,' I told her between wet snivels that dissolved into shouts and whoops.

The next morning, I sneaked up to the terrace, hid behind the water tank and shared a hurried cigarette with Raj, my younger brother. Soon, it was time and I shyly asked Sunny to set the code for the number locks to his birthday. The new Samsonite suitcases, with new sweaters for London, were hauled into the SUV.

The suitcases bobbed as Raj ignored potholes and rocketed down the road. Sunny sat in the front, his hands clutching the dashboard. I sat at the back next to Ma and Daddyji. My head was on Ma's shoulder. She stroked my hair softly and said, 'Be like sugar. Dissolve into your new home and make it a sweeter place.'

When I passed through immigration in London, I switched to the American accent that I had been trained to use at the call centre. I would sound more impressive, I thought, like I travelled abroad all the time. Sunny doubled over with laughter while we waited at the luggage belt and I slapped him, giggling, on his shoulder.

Sunny took me to a nightclub, because he knew how much I wanted to go but I couldn't wear the short metallic skirt I'd bought. I felt embarrassed at the thought of wearing it in front of my mother-in-law.

The day Sunny went back to work it struck. I'm not on holiday.

I live here. And that's when we began cooking every day, Asthma and me. I call Sunny's mom Asthma. It's because she makes me feel breathless and not in the 'I just spotted Shahrukh Khan on Oxford Street' sort of way.

Sunny is her darling son. If he rushes to work, skipping breakfast, she worries all day about him being hungry. She rings him precisely at one thirty every afternoon to check whether he has eaten lunch. The first question she asks him when he gets home is, 'Beta, should I make you a roti?' If he goes towards the fridge, she jumps up like Daler Mehndi in an enthu dance move and asks what he wants to eat. She spends her days cooking for him and in the afternoons, she watches Kung-Fu movies.

Now that Sunny is a married man, Asthma wants to make sure that I will care for him in the same way she does. Not in a near about same way or a slightly different way but in the exact same way. The food has to be made just like she makes it, with the same combination and proportion of masalas. If I make it any other way, she sings, 'Looks like something new is being made,' through narrow letterbox eyes. She then tastes it and tells her me how I ought to have made it.

I told Sunny I'm going mental, crack and fully mad.

'You'll get a job soon, darling, and then it won't matter so much,' he said squeezing my hand. 'Try and ignore her?' But, it was much harder than I thought. I kept sending out applications and no one replied.

I took the bus to Tesco. I always take the bus to the big Tesco when I want privacy. I called my mother who heard the whole *ram kahani* and said, 'Have a baby beti, everything will be all right then.' I hung up on her.

When I returned, Asthma switched off the *hi-yah, hi-yah* movie. I imagined her jumping up and kicking her feet in the air with a whoop, and bit down on an escaped giggle. 'Good movie?' I queried, arranging my face into a polite smile as I flopped down on the sofa. I flipped open the magazine I'd picked up from the shop with Kate Middleton on the cover.

'Arre, today's was just wonderful! *Mazza aa gaya*!' Asthma exclaimed, clapping her hands. 'To fight like the master, become the master!'

I smiled and started flicking through the pages of the magazine.

'Kung-Fu holds all of life's secrets. If I was younger, I would learn it,' she exclaimed. I looked up, startled.

She was looking me up and down, her searchlight gaze making me nervous. 'Oh look, you're wearing the same colour as me.'

I looked down at my purple suit and then at hers and nodded fake-enthusiastically.

'To fight like the master, become the master!' she muttered, eyes glittering like Diwali lights.

'*Haan*!' she bellowed, tugging at the ring on her finger, a ruby circled by twinkling diamonds. It slowly loosened and with a last strenuous pull, came off the bulging knuckle. She placed it on the table. It was the emerald's turn next; the one the astrologer from India had sent her to ward off the depression that had descended when her husband died of a heart attack three years ago. After several minutes of screwing up her face and wrenching, Asthma collapsed against the sofa. '*Ja mar*!' she cursed, scurrying to the bathroom where she lathered her hands into a soapy frenzy so that her fingers became slippery and the ring clinked into the ceramic sink.

She marched back brandishing it triumphantly. She slapped it down on the table next to the ruby. Finally, she took off her thick gold bangle.

I watched her actions surreptitiously, over the magazine.

'These are for you to wear.'

I lowered the magazine slowly, placed it on my lap and looked at her with an uncertain frown.

'Oh ho don't look so confused, just wear them,' she rapped.

Not wanting to offend her, I picked up the ruby like it was a baby alien. I hesitantly slipped it on my fattest finger. I lifted my hand to show her the ring, although I wasn't sure what this was about. Was she gifting her jewellery to me?

'Good, good, now the rest.'

Hands and wrist bedecked with the rings and bangle, I followed her into the kitchen. I stared at the blurry bangle as I wiped my stinging eyes while chopping the onions in preparation for the evening meal. I looked at her pouring oil into the wok. She looked back at me.

'Come here,' she said.

I lifted the chopping board with the moon-shaped onions on it and went towards her.

'Put these down.'

I followed her instructions dutifully. The chopping board was deposited on the black, granite ledge, next to the chopped tomatoes and boiled chickpeas. Asthma took off her purple and white striped chiffon scarf and draped it around my neck. I looked down at it, forehead creasing.

'Look at your hands,' she said.

I gazed down at them. They looked so strange with my mother-in-law's jewellery, like they weren't my hands at all. The jewellery

28

was an older woman's, large and ornate. My tastes ran to the delicate.

'Now close your eyes and imagine that your hands are actually my hands.'

Alarmed, my eyes popped open.

'Shut, shut them. Imagine, feel it,' commanded Asthma.

'Now when you cook, let your hands be mine,' she whispered in a silky slither. 'If you actually, *actually* feel it, your hands will know exactly what to do. Come, open your eyes,' she said in her Kung-Fu master voice.

Her rapturous face swam like a reflection upon water.

'Don't look so fearful. Just do as I say. Your hands are my hands. Yes?'

I nodded my head.

'Good. So, today I am not going to tell you what to do. My hands will guide you from within.'

A chair scraped past kitchen tiles and she plopped down. 'To be the mummy, cook like the mummy.' She smiled smugly.

I cooked the meal wearing a purple suit like my mother-in-law's with the two ends of her purple and white chiffon scarf hanging down my back. My hands felt disconnected from my body as I stirred the chickpea curry. They looked like robot hands, horror movie hands. I pined for the shower.

I stretched my arms and arched my back. I stood in the shower stall, naked but for the metallic mini skirt hugging my hips. I rested my back against the cold tiles and slowly slid to the ground. My breathing deepened, I closed my eyes and lay there. I slid further till I was lying on the ground, my hands under my head and feet up on the gleaming levers. I slowly turned the lever to the right with my feet, excitement gathering in my stomach, shivers running up and down my spine. The hot water rained down. I lifted my face to meet it and waited. Waited to turn into myself.

FOX CUB

CG Menon

Kumar doesn't know it, but today is the last time he will hide jewellery for his daughter.

His breath smokes as he kneels by the chest of drawers in the spare room, his fingers purple with cold. He burrows through a jumble of cassettes and old keys, adding the bangles to a heap of jewellery at the bottom. He'd bought a bangle for Meena too, that she'd shoved under her rolled-up cardigan. There'd been snow earlier – the first they'd seen – and it had made her furtive and scurrying, as though the sky had turned over and opened one lazy eye in her direction.

He'd bought the bangles yesterday, trying to fill his yawning lunch break. He's never been brave enough to join the other cashiers, thronging the park tables in a jumble of scarves and smiles. He tries, every day, but loses heart and skulks away to the canal instead. A group of girls loiter there in silence, tipping their pushchairs back and forth on the concrete rim. They handle their children like baggage, waiting for the park to empty again. By midday there's always a hard light bouncing from the water and glancing off the women's faces, turning them into statues with nothing to say for themselves.

Yesterday he'd walked right up to them, his lips gummed with spit and the taste of their spray-on perfume. They'd pivoted away when he came near, spinning about on the axis of their oversized prams. They were clumsy and large-hipped, but disappointment had pooled like water in his gut as he watched them walk away. The mall behind them was grim – a parade of hardware-shoes-drycleaners-stationery – and he'd marched straight through as his breath slowed and the ache between his legs began to fade to a guilty warmth. By the time he'd found the bangles in a shabby, half-carpeted jewellers, he'd convinced himself that those speechless girls didn't, after all, matter.

He flexes his fingers. Since they arrived four months ago, his skin's been shrivelling back from the nails. It's the cold, he tells himself, and kneels in the spare room, watching his palms turn the colour of Thrissur's jacarandas. Downstairs, Meena chivvies idlis from a pan. She works hard, he admits with a kind of guilty generosity. She cooks with white flour when she can't buy gram, she wipes the seeping kitchen drains, she keeps her smiles and loses her babies. The last miscarriage was two months ago.

Kumar walks downstairs and into the kitchen, where he whisks a tea towel off the rack. He doesn't ask her how she's feeling, in case she tells him. He imagines those babies ribboning out of her rosy mouth. And everything else spooling after them; the way her bones crumble when he leaves in the morning, the way everything fades in the pale gleam of sunset, and the way his jacaranda fingers try to stick her back together at night with jewellery.

Instead he says, 'The idlis are good.' They are. He has nothing to complain of.

At night he holds her, their breath leaping into mist on the windowpanes. He can see the dark row of terraced houses from his pillow with an occasional light glowing in an attic room. It looks like something from his schoolboy Dickens, but in the thin slices of alleyways he can see foxes slipping by. Dickens never mentioned foxes, and this worries him. He wonders what else is coming.

As Meena sleeps, Kumar sends out tendrils to the mean corners of the house. If they were still in Thrissur, there would be people in those corners – aunties and brothers and Meena's Amma and Appa – all of them pushing back the dark with invisible balloons of breath. But here there's only him, and whatever is left of Meena tonight, and the foxes outside in the dark.

Except, of course, for his daughter. His ghostly daughter, the only one who'd lived long enough to be born at all. They've brought her with them from Thrissur somehow, caught up in the striped handles of their bags, trapped in the spare room drawers and under Meena's tongue. He smiles at the thought. If he has to be haunted by a little ghost – a never-was – then he's glad it's her. He turns over, pushing cold hands between his thighs where his scrotum hangs like a bag of milk. Stay warm, little one, he thinks, and dreams of tiny purple fists stiffened with gold.

Next morning, the bus station feels more crowded than usual. Kumar climbs onto the bus and joins the usual commuters, all filed neatly in their suits and hung from the strap rail. From the window, he looks back at the benches crammed with sleeping people. Asleep in their dirty puffer jackets and ripped sleeping bags, lining the edges of all that cavernous, whistling space. He was used to beggars in Thrissur, but it shocked him to find them here. They're like the foxes, the sneaking snow and the blank young women with their lumpish hips. All of them are too quiet for their own good.

It's late by the time he finishes work. The streets have been dark for hours and the other clerks have left, each pulling on gloves and muffling up a neck scarred with acne or stubble. Kumar looks up each time, smiles and reaches for his own scarf.

'I'll join you, just wait, is it?' he says to each one.

But they all hurry out, giving him exaggerated, matey sort of waves and letting the door slam. Again and again Kumar replaces his scarf and wipes the hope from his face.

By six, he's the last one left. The office looks brighter and more secretive, and he moves about it as though cast in a play. He sits at the other desks, touches the drawers and examines photographs. Most of the pictures are of children: birthday parties and swimming pools and graduations. When he switches the lights off to leave, those dusky paper smiles glimmer back at him from the shadows.

The streets outside are frozen, their flaking asphalt covered with a thin, grey slush. By the time he reaches the bus stop, the air's full of ice and a spiky cold has lodged in his ribs.

There's a girl waiting, pasty under the yellowing street light. She looks Indian – paler than he is, maybe Punjabi. Her shiny pink jacket is torn at the cuffs and grimy with wear. Despite the cold he can smell her, a sweetish stink like bins in summer.

'Got any change?'

He jumps. Her voice is high and a little blurred, as though she's calling from a moving train.

'I ...yes, I have just some.' He fumbles a hillock of pennies into her cupped hand and she closes her fingers with a sudden, luminous smile. The plastic beads around her wrist rattle as she moves, and he swallows.

'I don't mean to... I'm sorry... but...why don't you go home?'

She doesn't answer, just looks up at him. The dirt seems to lie on her skin like an eggshell glaze. It's not right, he thinks suddenly. She should be dressed in a satin party-frock and smiling for the camera at a birthday or graduation. Under that dirt, she's the cleanest person he's ever seen.

'Nowhere to go, is it?' she says. Her voice bites at something inside him and to his surprise he hears himself answer.

'Come with me. For tonight, I mean. My wife will look after you.'

She screws her face up. 'What? Fuck off!'

He hadn't expected the language, spilling into the gluey, half-frozen air but he's almost pleased. Meena keeps – in another spare room drawer she thinks he doesn't know about – a stash of pages ripped from parenting magazines. How To Cope With Teenagers. Talking To Your Child. He's read them over and over, creeping back on quiet, sun-slanted afternoons to sit cross-legged and wistful on the carpet.

When the girl stops swearing, he opens his wallet and plucks out a photograph.

'This is my wife,' he says, and again, 'she'll look after you.'

It's a good photo, showing Meena with her years-ago smile. The girl takes it by the edges with a shy delicacy.

'OK,' she shrugs, and slides the photograph into the back pocket of her jeans. 'Too cold to sleep out anyway.'

She unfurls like a crane, all legs and feathers she hasn't quite grown into yet. He'd like the photo back but doesn't know how to ask so he buttons his coat and tries a fatherly smile.

'Come,' he says. 'The bus will be here.'

She waits for him to buy her a ticket, then props herself against him on the stiff-bristled seat. Someone nudges her, asks if her father could close the window, and Kumar shudders with an aching kind of pride.

As they wait together, her fingers turn a delicate blue. She tells him she's fifteen years old; that she's called Nita; that she hasn't eaten today. She has a smile like Meena's and hands like his own, and she's as unsettling as snow.

Meena's anger puffs fine wisps of hair to float above her scalp. They're arguing in whispers while Nita has a shower.

'Why did you bring her here? A beggar-girl like that.'

'It's cold, Meena,' he tries to explain, but she slaps that away, knocks over one of the water glasses he's set out. The glass smashes in the sink and Meena glares as if he's let something leggy and scuttling into her world.

'Just for one night,' he begs. He tells her that Nita has nowhere to go. He tries to explain about the way she cupped her hands for the pennies, about the gloss and shine of her under all that dirt. Meena shrugs her shoulders and turns back to the stove.

'She'll steal from us,' she tells him in a dry voice. 'Or she'll think you're after something else.'

There's a giggle and he looks up to see Nita leaning against the doorway. Her hair's shining and she smells of conditioner.

She's put her old clothes back on, right down to the grimy jacket, and her sweet-sharp stink creeps out. They'll need to lend her pyjamas.

She stretches, still leaning against the door, and pops a nub of chewing gum in her mouth. The gum makes her look as if she's talking, chattering away to ghosts or angels or his own little never-was daughter. Sisters always do share secrets, he thinks, and yearns for whispered confidences, homework, shared clothes and pop songs fizzing behind closed bedroom doors.

'I'm Nita,' she says, And then, in a sing-song voice like something she's learnt at school, 'Thank you for having me.'

Meena isn't convinced, he can tell. She doesn't believe in the scrubbed glow of Nita's ears or her well-behaved hair. He watches his wife ladle out three platefuls of dal with cauliflower, careful to make them equal.

'Please, eat,' she tells them both.

Kumar hesitates, under the jumpy blue-white kitchen light that turns Meena's face cruel and Nita's sly. He turns the light off, pulling down the orange glass shade instead, and the three of them huddle in that pool of amber. Nita keeps chewing her gum while they eat. Kumar wants to tell her to stop – she's spoiling the taste of the food, it isn't respectful, it isn't right – but he doesn't know how. She's become more distant, looking away from him in the yellowish light. There's a slipping-aside secrecy in the turn of her head, as though she's finding the gaps and edges in things.

'Thank you for dinner,' she says, after a few more minutes of silence. 'It was delicious.'

She's barely touched it – dabbed her spoon around a little, that's all – and her hands lie insolently in her lap. Kumar stops eating, embarrassed by the sound of his own chewing. Under the table he feels Meena's disbelief judder his knees.

'Nita… if you're finished, I mean… would you like to go to bed?' A shred of cauliflower lodges against his gums and he works at it with his tongue. 'Meena will make you up a bed in the spare room.'

The spare room is cold, it's unpainted and dusty with a lonely radiator spitting tepid air. No place for a child, he thinks. Not a real child or even a never-was and a never-will-be. Nita and Meena trail out of the room, and Kumar isn't crying, not really, he's only switching the radio on and cleaning up the shattered glass in the sink. Take care tonight, the announcer urges, it's going to be cold. Cold enough to freeze pipes, to break windows and water-glasses and pry daughters away from their fathers' arms.

Meena comes back down with a practical, things-on-my-mind curl to her lips. He'd like to talk but he isn't sure how well sound carries in this house. He whispers instead and tiptoes around with exaggerated care. Meena washes up with no noise at all and he wonders if this is how she spends all her days, moving on the edge of her breath in case someone overhears.

In bed that night, his belly shrinks away from Meena's sleeping back. He thinks of Nita, across the hall with his own little ghost, both of them wary and out of place. He hopes Nita isn't scared. He hopes she's fast asleep, with her chewing gum left to harden quietly under the bannisters or on a window-ledge where he'll paint over it years later on a sunlit morning.

When he wakes, there's a stormy, curdled light in the room. He still hasn't got the hang of mornings here, that shock of cold and the greyish air that smells of everything shut-in and breathed-out.

Downstairs, he pours porridge into a saucepan and plans their polite goodbyes. *Thank you for having me. So glad you could come.* Nita's blue-tinged hands, the front door shutting as Meena washes her silent dishes, and foxes curl through the alleys outside.

'Nita,' he calls softly as he walks upstairs. He feels new-hatched, stumbling and blind as though he's squinting into a glare.

Nita isn't in the spare room. The window's open and the bed hasn't been slept in. He isn't surprised by that, nor the pile of rubbish where she's emptied the chest of drawers out on the floor. The jewellery is gone, all the bangles and chains and trinkets. Only one tiny glass earring's left, hooked into a spooled-out cassette tape. *Go safely, little one*, he thinks, *stay warm*, and tucks the earring into his palm.

It isn't until he's picked everything up that he finds Meena's photograph, right at the bottom. Nita must have wiped it clean. She's put a shred of sticky-tape on a ripped edge and smoothed out the creases. Meena looks younger with the paper frown marks erased from her eyes. In the corner of the drawer, jamming it open forever, there's a hardened blob of chewing gum.

Kumar sits back on his heels. He can smell the porridge burning downstairs amid the scraps and ends of silence. Perhaps, he thinks, this is how daughters break your heart.

MIGRATION

Mona Dash

The Banyan tree and the Oak
know the same language

Migration
is not an answer
nor a question
Movement
birds leave and return

Passport engraved with a stamp
coloured, dated. I
booked a ticket, landed in a country
closer to the poles from a country
closer to the equator

I didn't know
I would collect theories and words
on my back
like a feathery creature

feathers firm on the body
plucking one out
draws blood

Wonder why, how, I became
so many things at once
Emigrant, Immigrant, Migrant, Subaltern
theories to luxuriate, nest in

I didn't know
that I am invisible
when I enter a room

I didn't know
the philosophers, post-colonists
have labelled behaviour
branded my very soul
Hybridity, Provincialism, Orientalism
my shadows, my silhouettes defined
before I knew

Two-headed Janus
looking out, looking in
from where we came
to where we came

I didn't know
I thought i was I
I was i

First published in The Lake, UK (May 2018)

IMPLICATIONS

Mona Dash

Born and raised an Indian; not living in India

implied: *not Indian*

now British, not born in Britain

implied: *not British*

a mother, working full-time

implied: *not a mother*

a sales manager, also a mother

implied: *not a sales manager*

a woman, a mother

implied: *not a woman*

a writer, working in technology

implied: *not a writer*

an engineer, also an artist

implied: *not an engineer*

a businessperson, also a poet

implied: *not a businessperson*

becoming more than I was meant to

implied: *a sense of erosion*

Venn-diagram like I seek

                         Implied: *commonalities*

finding intersectionality

                            Implied: *a pinpoint*

A SIMPLE MAN

Reshma Ruia

My sister calls me from Birmingham. Suddenly. Out of the blue. We haven't spoken for months and here she is at the end of the phone.

'Pikku, I am coming to London to stay with you. I have problems at home.'

Her voice quivers as though she's speaking under water.

She pauses before continuing. 'Are you able to look after me?'

I know what she's asking. Can I support her? What could I say? She's my younger sister and she needs me.

'Of course, Bubbly,' I reply. 'Come and stay for as long as you want. I have a good job and I make enough.'

She lets out a long sigh of relief. 'Thank God for that. I know London is a costly city and I was worried that you wouldn't have a proper job.'

I knew what she meant by 'proper'. A job like my father's, sitting in a big office with important files on the desk and a secretary busy taking notes.

'I have a proper job,' I said, warily.

'I knew you would land on your feet one day. I am so proud of you,' she said, as though I am a bird that has finally laid a golden egg.

Bubbly has been here for several days. I'm trying to distract her from her constant requests to visit me at work. It's a game that's becoming tedious and worrying.

'I would love to look around your office,' she says again, like a child clamouring to visit a toyshop. She calls it that even though I've explained that I work in a museum and although I have responsibilities, my duties aren't strictly professional. One day, someday soon, I will have to tell her the truth about my modest job that can barely pay the bills but for now I'm enjoying basking in the glow of her admiration.

On Sunday she declares it's the perfect day for a visit. It is summer and it isn't raining. We would get off the tube at Waterloo, cross the metal bridge that bows beneath the weight of hurrying feet and begin our walk, strolling along the pavement that runs beside the river, not talking, but enjoying the sunshine warming our faces. Peace in our souls.

Wear something colourful for a change, I almost say to Bubbly, not your usual uniform of black sweatshirt and leggings but I don't want to disrespect her sorrow, the sorrow of a woman who has lost her husband. Bubbly is the baby of the family. When I look at her, I don't see a woman with greying hair and sloping shoulders who sucks in her cheeks when she is thinking hard, I see a plump-faced child in a lacy frock doing somersaults in our parents' garden in Kampala. The servants, Igbo, Homer, even old Mwamba the gardener are in a circle around her. They clap their

45

hands and sway their heads, singing out her name as she flips over and over and rolls down the hill. The wind stirs the trees so that the white and pink flowers of the Coral tree fall over her head like a blessing.

Much has changed. Kampala is now just a name on a map. Today, Bubbly is a widow who has left her family home in Birmingham because she's fallen out with her son and his wife. It happens. One minute she is happily settled, the next minute she is on my doorstep, suitcase in hand. She has enrolled for an accountancy course through the Open University.

Bubbly is the clever one of the family. Me, I'm just a simple man. 'A dunce who will never amount to much. A simpleton,' my father snarled when I didn't get the grades to get into college in England. Even on his deathbed, he'd turned his head to Bubbly, gripped her fingers and promised her she would fly high. Bless your son too, my mother cried, pushing me towards his slowly dying face, but the light in his eyes dimmed and the doctor hushed us into silence.

Our Sunday afternoon walk soon brings us to the museum. There it stands, a concrete block that hugs the curve of the river's lip like a mole. The swollen white clouds floating above are mirrored in its shiny glass panes. Bubbly can't make up her mind whether it's beautiful or ugly.

'Maybe it's ugly in a beautiful way, *bhaiya*,' she says, eyes narrowed, her fingers drumming her chin.

I told you she is the smart one.

'It used to be a power station,' I explain. 'They want it to reflect its heritage, that's why it's so brutal looking.' I had stolen these lines from the visitors' pamphlets that lay in a pile at the museum entrance.

Bubbly nods her head, impressed. 'Now, let's see your room. I bet you have a big desk and an Apple computer.' Her voice rises in excitement.

'You think I have such a computer. And a big office?' I touch her hand and my eyes almost well up.

'Of course. Why wouldn't you, Pikku? Never underestimate yourself.' There she goes, wagging her finger like a schoolteacher.

I say it's too complicated to get us into the museum. She will have to get a pass, sign forms. 'Let's leave it for another day.'

She nods and pats my hand understandingly.

'Whenever you are ready,' she says, as we head back.

I am so lucky to have her as my sister. But the truth is I am ashamed. Ashamed to tell her I am just a humble guard who patrols the large rooms. I was lucky to get the job without any qualifications. Unlike other men of my age, I don't possess much but I am satisfied. I call myself the guardian angel of these paintings. Every day from nine to five, I stand at the door, watching the crowds shuffle past paintings, pause, shift, clear their throats, take furtive photos on their mobile phones until I walk across to them and warn them in a whisper loud enough for the room to hear, 'No flash photography please.' I press my index finger against my mouth and shake my head but always with a smile. I don't want to hurt their feelings.

I am too busy to notice the paintings, much like a harassed mother with her brood of children, too busy head counting to notice the odd sniveling or tummy cramp. Instead, I stare at the visitors. They arrive, heads strapped to their audio guides, hands gripping phones, brochures, notebooks.

On Monday mornings, we get a briefing from the boss.

'Watch out for the rucksacks and the prams,' he shouts.

Single young men who linger too long before a particular painting, or whose hands dive into their pockets and spring out a camera are dangerous. I must walk over to them, my navy blue uniform announcing its authority, the walkie-talkie itching in my hand ready to leap into action. The boss comes close and jabs my shoulder with his thumb. 'You, you straw head. Are you listening? Don't start daydreaming about your Banglaland or wherever you come from, OK? Keep your eyes open.' His breath stinks of bacon. The other guards giggle and I laugh along with them. He means well. These paintings cost millions and I am their caretaker. My chest swells with pride.

Four years of service and I have seen them all. Rich, poor, the down at heel who use the museum to shelter from the cold and the lonely playing mating games within these walls. There are regulars who are almost friends. We exchange smiles and a wave. There's the mother who comes every Friday afternoon with her teenage daughter, apple cheeked and strong limbed. Arm in arm they stride from picture to picture, talking in excited whispers. It must be nice to have such a close mother daughter bond.

Then there is the Japanese gentleman who comes in a suit and tie, probably works in a bank. He carries a briefcase and a camera and pauses before each painting, looks in my direction, gives a slight bow of the head and takes the shot. I can't really shout at him because he's so gentle so I choose that moment to bend down and tie my shoelace or whisper a quick greeting to my colleague, Reginald, who is patrolling the next room.

'How is it going, bro?' I ask.

'I feel like a Pope in a brothel,' he replies, laughing.

Reginald is from Guyana but has Indian blood swimming somewhere deep inside him. For years, he's been pestering me to invite him home. 'Man, I want your curries, your roti meat,' he says, his voice wheedling with want. Maybe one of these days, I will bring him some of Bubbly's samosas but no way am I bringing him home to meet her. He has dirty eyes.

I wonder why people visit a museum. What do they want to see as they shuffle timidly past and stand respectfully in front of the paintings, eyes devouring the colour, squinting at the labels, looking for meaning. Is it something they can't find inside the arms of their loved ones or outside in the parks or in the temples and churches?

Bubbly has cooked my favourite childhood dish, *luwombo* with smoked chicken and plantain leaf. She shakes her head when I tell her how the people stand with open mouths in front of paintings of dead, pink and white kings and queens.

'Why should they rule us even after they are gone?' I ask her.

She says people are always looking for leaders to hold their hand, even if they end up with their hands chopped off. 'Just like Big Daddy Idi Amin.'

We say the name together and start grinning even though what he did to us was not very funny.

'I bet you're a good boss. A good leader to your team. I wish father was alive and he could see you,' she says, squeezing my arm. I fall silent.

Sometimes the museum turns into a party place for the rich and the important. A quiet hush descends on the museum on such nights, the lights dim and smartly dressed young women arrive, their arms filled with white roses and trays of tea lights. There is the rustle of stiff white table cloths swung over the trestle tables that are wheeled in for the occasion. I offer to help but the young Polish men say they've got it under control. Then the speeches begin. It's a pleasant drone that I don't even attempt to follow but some words stick out – *abstract* is one and *sensory impact* another. I will look them up in Bubbly's dictionary. My eyelids turn heavy as the voices carry on and to keep myself awake I try to spot the Indians. The men fiddle with their mobile phones and the women give me a glance and then look away, ashamed that one of their own is doing such a menial job. Once, an Indian lady had carelessly dropped her shawl. I scooped it up and gave it to her. '*Yeh lijiye…*' I used my politest Hindi as I offered it to her but she was having none of it. Chin tilted in defiance and without so much as a thank you, she snatched it from me.

Reginald and I always volunteer to do double duty on such nights. It's an easy way to earn overtime, watch the rich as they eat and drink.

'Like bloody monkeys in a zoo,' Reginald whispers as he walks past me to take up his spot.

The girls glide around, holding titbits in decorative papier-mâché bowls. My stomach rumbles. How is it that the rich are never hungry?

These gatherings bring back the old days in Kampala when the autumn breeze had shooed away the last of the summer heat and the red dust on the roads had settled down. Father threw dinner parties for the Very Important Parasites or VIPs. That's what he called them. The house hummed with the sound of running feet and moving hands, and mother shouting out orders to the servants in her thin reedy voice.

'Make sure you grate the ginger, not cut it in such thick slices. Is the mutton already cooked? Where is the lace table cloth?'

Her voice travels across the lost years to find me on such evenings and I am grateful for the memory.

I would watch the ministers pull up in their long, sleek, white cars with flashing lights on the roof. Just as I was about to run to the gate to greet them, father's strong arms swooped me up.

'Where do you think you're going? Stay quiet in your room. Don't you dare come out and embarrass me, you dunce.' Bubbly welcomed the guests instead of me, reciting her nursery rhymes without forgetting a single word. The ministers patted her head and said she was a clever child.

'There is a new exhibition opening in your office,' Bubbly says one day. 'They're having a major exhibition of an Indian painter. I read about it in the newspaper. He is called Atul Ghose.'

I feel my muscles tense when she says this. I'm supposed to know such things.

'Oh yes…of course.' Like a parrot, I repeat what I've heard the curator say. I may have a slow mind, but I also have quick ears.

Bubbly gives me a hug, her head with its thin, sparse hair pressed against my chest. 'My clever, clever brother. I am so proud of you,' she whispers, her quiet eyes beaming through her steel framed spectacles.

When I come back after the weekend, the walls of the museum are plastered with bold new posters. They show an Indian man with a goatee beard and sallow, aubergine-coloured smoker's lips. *Atul Ghose, the Enigma of Parting. Portraits of an Age.* That's what the posters say. I take out my little notebook and jot down, *enigma.* One more word to add to my vocabulary. Seeing that Indian face with its brown sunken cheeks and the inky shadows under the eyes makes me happy. I don't know why. It just does. My chest puffs out in pride when Reginald and I sit together in the canteen for lunch.

'Say Reginald, can you name me some painters from Guyana?' I ask him innocently.

He shakes his head. 'Nope cannot. This art business is a white man's game. Empty bellies have no time to paint.' His face looks momentarily sad and then clears up. 'It's all bullshit anyway, man.'

'We have painters in India,' I correct him. 'In fact if you care to look at the walls rather than scratching your balls, you will see one. Atul Ghose is his name.'

'Is that so?' Reginald says. Eyes round like the moon. 'There are so many billions of you shits anyway, one of them was bound to end up with a paint brush.' He shrugs dismissively and turns to his egg-mayo sandwich.

The morning of the opening, I make sure my uniform jacket is finely pressed. The room is already buzzing by the time I arrive for my shift and take up my position. Clever types in black walk backwards and forwards, eyes narrowed into slits, punching furiously into their iPads and mobiles. The crowds finally thin in the late afternoon. It's been a bright day and sunlight steals through the protective blinds of the museum windows and brightens the room. I leave my post by the door and walk closer to the paintings. Let's see what this Atul Ghose is about.

The beauty. It stabs me right in the heart. Men and women crowd the canvas, colourful like a peacock's plumage, deep in embrace. The night above them is sprinkled with a dusting of stars. Cows mew at their reflection in a pond flooded with lotus flowers. I read the title underneath the painting, *Krishna's love tryst with his gopis. Tryst,* I jot in my book. I move to the next painting of a naked couple, arms entwined, sitting on a swing made of woven flowers. A dog prowls nearby, nibbling their toes. My face grows hot in embarrassment. Has the painter no shame? I look around, furtive. No one is watching, so I extend my finger and lightly brush it against the woman's exposed breast.

I find it difficult to sleep that night.

'It's that green tea you gave me,' I shout to Bubbly through my open door. 'Rubbish,' she snorts. 'It must be the beer you have been drinking with your colleagues.'

She means Reginald of course. Her bedroom is opposite mine, and we sleep, our single beds positioned so we can see each other's faces as we lie in bed, chatting until our eyelids grow heavy with sleep. I dream of elephants that night and of young bare-breasted girls dancing under a canopy of stars. When I wake up next day, the day is flat and grey like a dead fish.

Atul Ghose is a success. I turn up for work and there is already a queue snaking past the museum shop, right up to the cafeteria. The crowds can't get enough of his blue-skinned Krishna and dancing ladies.

'Well done on getting him,' Bubbly says one evening. She has been reading up on the exhibition. I wish she would focus on her accountancy papers, but no, she has to ask me a thousand questions about Atul Ghose. I tell her how he lives all alone on a farm in France and walks barefoot everywhere.

'I would like to see his paintings,' Bubbly says.

'That's not possible. All the tickets are sold out.' I don't want her to see me in my guard's uniform.

Her mouth turns down in disappointment and then reshapes into a smile.

'Don't worry about it, Pikku,' she says, tenderly. 'Maybe you can get me the catalogue.'

I look at her closely, trying to read her face like a map. How much does she know? This would be the perfect time to tell her about my job. Tell her that I don't sit behind a big desk shouting orders. But, a voice inside me whispers, *Don't tell her, she will be disappointed*. I decide to bring Atul Ghose home to her. I will borrow the painting of Krishna and Gopis show it to her and replace it. Simple. No more pestering, only pride in her brother.

I tell no one at work about my genius plan. The hours seem to drag slowly that day and I can hear the drumbeat of my heart. At a certain point in the evening, the lights dim and the PA system coughs into life, urging the visitors to gather their belongings and leave because the museum is about to shut. Footsteps start retreating like waves leaving the shore. And then there is silence. I walk up to the painting, pull out a pair of scissors from my pocket. Snip. It is done. The painting falls into my arms. I tuck it under my armpit and begin the walk to the exit.

There is noise, a wailing whistle and flashing lights.

'What the fuck are you doing, man?' Reginald shouts as he spots me.

I begin running.

LOST AND FOUND

Shibani Lal

'Definitely a virgin,' leers Fat Fred, pointing at the cranberry-red trolley case. It sparkles with innocent, fresh-out-of-the-tin promise, and I want it, but since Fred's spotted it, he gets first dibs.

'Reckon you'll get it, easy. Hardly anyone here,' I say, scanning the saleroom. 'We're the only regulars today.'

'Them?' he points towards a Japanese couple in the far corner.

'More likely to piss their pants than bid,' I chuckle. 'Check out that dude.' I tilt my head toward a posh-looking chap lurking by the entrance, incongruous in head-to-toe tweed.

'Bloody hell,' Fred grunts. 'Bet he's a pouf.'

'Point is; I doubt he'll put up a fight.' I continue studying the room. There are a few others scattered about like forgotten cigarette butts, but I suspect they're here in a purely ornamental capacity.

'Heck, yeah,' grins Fred. 'Might get this baby dead cheap.'

'Nothing else worth going for today,' I say, looking through the bags.

'Last coupla auctions have been pretty shit,' Fred nods.

'Standard's falling. Been ages since we had a really good lot, 'bout time Greasby's stepped up. Come on, she's here.' He gives the auctioneer an ingratiating smile as we walk towards our seats. She ignores him.

I scan the room once more before removing my sunglasses. I've never met anyone I know here, and I doubt I will, but that doesn't stop me from checking, just to be sure. I'd be mortified if it happened, although I'm not sure why, since there's nothing particularly salacious about a used-luggage auction. And whilst I can't speak for the others – Fat Fred, Hairy Paul, Greasy John, I'm fairly certain they cradle Greasby's close to their chests too. We've nothing in common really, apart from this nondescript auction house, and we float in and out of here, never knowing when we're going to see each other again; if at all. Our lives don't intersect beyond the sanctity of these walls and we wouldn't have it any other way.

I had chanced upon Greasby's a couple of years ago when I was reading my horoscope in the Evening Standard on the bus home – *The sun in Jupiter will see you traveling to exotic destinations!* – when the line 'Lesser known-auction houses' caught my eye. I turned my attention to the article – *Uranus will bring sudden changes your way!* Greasby's was included at the end, with perhaps the same reluctance with which one invites the quiet new girl at school with the thick-set glasses to a party. But then the girl turns out to be rather good fun and suddenly, life without her is no longer the same. In much the same way, I'd never considered the fate of all those unclaimed bags languishing at Heathrow before, but the thought of bidding for them at an auction consumed me for days. I went for my first auction after a few weeks of dithering, and it's been a pleasant addiction ever since.

My first win, several months later, was a slightly battered, tadpole-green suitcase.

'Found anything?' asked Fred glancing over my shoulder.

'Dirty laundry, a travel iron, couple of pairs of jeans and six stilettos.'

'Shucks,' muttered Hairy Paul.

'Loving the optimism, guys.' I snapped the bag shut. 'It's not going to happen.'

'Ya never know, Nik, there's always a chance they miss something. I could find a ring hidden deep in a jeans pocket, yeah. Some shit like that. Diamonds maybe. Or emeralds.'

'Fred's right. Met a guy coupla years ago, he found a watch in there...inside pocket of a jacket. Sold it for a couple hundred quid,' said John. 'Ya just never know.' He narrowed his eyes, 'Why do this otherwise?'

'Just, you know, for fun,' I shrugged. 'Get a kick from looking through people's stuff.'

Paul snorted.

'Bollocks,' muttered Fred. 'You're here same as us. To get lucky. Find a rich bugger's bag, and you may just. Them rich folk pack all sorta shit.'

'A rolled-up Caravaggio in a pair of jeans, maybe,' I teased.

'Yeah. A Cara-Cara...that's what. Ya just never know,' grunted Fred, his jowls wobbling with unbridled optimism.

Fred's enthusiasm hasn't waned despite the disappointments. To his credit, he's made a tidy profit by peddling the cases on eBay. I admire his tenacity. I simply couldn't be bothered. Once

I'm done rummaging through the contents, I dump the entire lot at the Oxfam near home, although I have held on to some of my more entertaining finds: an oversize t-shirt with the words *Good coffee makes me SHIT*, a lurid purple vibrator, a pair of silk pyjamas with Tony Blair's face embroidered on the seat and finally, my favourite so far, a bright pink inflatable sheep fished from deep within the bowels of a nondescript duffle bag. It turned out to be a pretty handy footrest.

'Lot number fifteen, red Delsey trolley case with mixed clothing, hosiery, accessories, a few as new,' yells the auctioneer. I don't see why she's shouting given we're sitting like obedient ducklings in the front row.

'Bloody loves the sound of her voice, yeah,' mutters Fat Fred in an audible whisper, raising his card. Someone chuckles and the auctioneer glares at him. No one else bids and she brings the gavel down with a satisfying *thwack*. A toothless half-moon of a grin spreads across Fred's face. He's bagged a nearly new suitcase for a tenner.

'Yeah!' he punches his dinner-plate sized hand in the air.

'Quiet!' she snaps.

The rest of the auction is a wash. The Japanese couple rush out halfway, tripping over their umbrellas. The only other bidder is the posh bloke who bids for the *'duffle bag containing items of gentlemen's underwear'*. Fred sniggers.

'Wanna come check this baby out?' he calls, trundling over with his case.

'Sure. Hey, fingers crossed for that Picasso,' I grin, watching Fred unzip the bag.

'India!' he exclaims, holding a sari between his hands. 'Bloody hell, ain't seen a bag from India before.' He dips his fingers back into the case.

I haven't either. I've had bags from Mexico and Laos, and once, an oversized, foul-smelling case from Burundi stuffed with bags of tea and rancid cheese.

'It's from Mumbai.'

'What?'

He grins, pointing to a dry-cleaning tag affixed to a shirt. 'Mumbai Deluxe dry cleaners. Lotsa rich chaps there.' He continues ferreting around, tossing clothes out onto the makeshift table.

My heart thuds within my chest. 'Mumbai?'

'Bet there's some old Maharaja's jewels,' mutters Fred. 'False bottom, yeah. Saw on the telly one time, how they smuggled antique crap out of India like that,' he mumbles, running his sausage fingers along the lining with near-surgical precision.

I lean over and take a deep breath. It's faint but undeniable, a definitive Indian smell that emanates from deep within the case that floats past me like a long-forgotten friendly ghost. It hooks me at once, the soft smell of rosewater, a hint of mothballs, lurking like opals in forgotten corners of the linen cupboard and the heady fragrance of incense and sandalwood. I lean back and close my eyes. I'm transported to the muggy evenings and warm nights spent beneath the folds of the mosquito net. A lick of salt on my lips, the fresh morning sea-spray that left briny kisses on my cheeks and made messy birds' nest tangles of my hair. Forgotten scents of a time long past, smells of a childhood.

Mine.

Fat Fred's obvious disappointment is mollified somewhat as he runs a practiced eye across the suitcase.

'Reckon I'll sell this baby for eighty, poss a hundred,' he chortles, rubbing his belly. The tattoo of the dragon stretched thin against his abdomen winks grotesquely at me before settling back within the confines of Fred's shirt. 'Soft as a baby's arse,' he chuckles, caressing the bag. 'Hey, whatcha doing, Nik?'

'Huh? N-nothing.'

'Think it smells like curry or what?' Fred snatches the sari from my hand and holds it against his nose. 'Can't smell nothing,' he grunts, tossing it into the case. 'Weirdo.'

'Sure. Whatever. Say Fred,' I say, my voice shriller than usual. 'Why don't I take the clothes and stuff off you? I'll drop them off at Oxfam on my way home.'

'Why?' he narrows his eyes suspiciously.

'Just, you know,' I shrug. 'Thought it'll help.'

'Weird. Ya, sure thing,' he shrugs. 'Suit yourself. Was gonna chuck it anyway. Lemme take this baby,' he zips the case and pulls on his jacket. 'See ya later, Nik,' he waves.

A final flash of crimson and he's gone.

We left in a flash too. Left everything behind in that smoky black carcass, with rivulets of blood bubbling through the cindery remains.

It was Bombay then. It became Mumbai in 1995, the same year I became Nik. But the real changes, for both Bombay and me, had happened long before then, way back in March 1993. We left the city that month, in a mad scramble to the airport, Papa shouting, Caesar barking and Mama tense, her lips sealed shut like the flaps of an envelope. And me, tripping over hurriedly packed suitcases and rubbing sticky blobs of sleep out of my eyes as Papa hurried me out the door.

'Hurry up, goddamn it, we need to leave!'

'Rabbity! Papa, Rabbity!'

'Come on. Hurry up, we'll buy you another one.'

'Caesar, what about Caesar?' I yelled.

'Shut up. Stoppit. Not now. Let's go. NOW.'

I punched his legs with my fists.

'STOP IT. I'M WARNING YOU.'

'Please, Papa. Caesar...Rabbity...Mona's party...mermaid dress...tomorrow...'

His hand cut through the muggy night air like a knife. *Thwack*. Again. *Thwack*.

'Please,' I sobbed. 'Pl-please...'

Mama pulled me towards her and carried me in her arms. The door slammed shut and I could hear Caesar's howls as we squashed ourselves into the waiting cab.

'Airport,' Papa snapped. '*Jaldi*. Come on, let's go, *jaldi*.'

'Ssh.' Mama held me close. 'Go to sleep. Ssh.'

I nestled my tear-stained face against the warm folds of her scarf and closed my eyes. And then we were in London.

Our curtains in Bombay were bottle-green, although somewhat bleached from the years of relentless sun. We never drew them, preferring to have a perennial view of the sea, a placid, chalky-grey pond for most of the year except for during the monsoon, when fierce winds whipped the waves into lashings of milky-white foam. And we'd sit by the window, Mama and I, drinking glasses of lemonade as the breeze blew warm kisses on our cheeks.

But that March, Papa wouldn't let us. *Draw the bloody curtains.*

'We can't take any chances,' he said, running his hands through his hair. 'They're coming for me,' he whispered.

Mama trembled with worry and Caesar whimpered in the corner. I didn't know who *they* were then, but I do now. I still don't see them as killers. They bounced me on their knees and bought me bottles of Gold-Spot, sugary orange fizz that I'd sip through a curly straw late into the night when Papa took me with him to shut the restaurant.

I loved the restaurants. Papa owned four, strung like beads across the southern tip of the city. They were uniform in their garishness, each with a black door and the sign: *Red Dragon: Fine Indian-Chinese Cuisine* painted in red across the top with the image of a fire-breathing dragon alongside. The biggest was the one by the Docks, tucked away in a secluded corner between the fish market and a row of crumbling colonial buildings. There, in the quiet underbelly of the city, Papa hosted them, his new friends, my Gold-Spot-giving friends. They bought me a Walkman for my birthday. Michael Jackson crooned over the crackle of the banknotes they slipped into Papa's eager palm in exchange for allowing them to store their stuff, no questions asked, in the storeroom, a sliver of space sliced away from the main bowl of the restaurant. The diners laughed, oblivious, clinking their glasses in between mouthfuls of curry-spiced noodles whilst across the dimly-lit corridor, our friends heaved misshapen bags into the restaurant.

The fatal contents of which they eventually used on a fateful Friday in March. Stuff that ignited, maimed and killed. Bombs that burst in busy bazaars; explosives hidden in forgotten cars that detonated in not-so-forgotten places. Windows shattered and smoke billowed from hollowed-out buildings, staining the sky black, and we cowered in our apartment, breathing in the charcoal-peppered air that snaked in from the gaps between the windows. The streets oozed blood for days and the smell of rancid flesh permeated the air. We watched, enveloped in fear, as terror wound its tentacles tight around our city. Gold Spot and car bombs, bubbles and body parts, hearts beating and silenced, all against the quiet melody of the waves that licked salt into the cracks on the rocks by the shore.

Our new friends – they scurried like rats in the sewers, the police nipping at their tails. In the days that followed, a dribble of news: one shot here, another arrested there. The ones who remained couldn't afford to take any chances: no proof of their involvement to remain. A few days later, they bombed the Red Dragon by the docks. One look at the smoky carcass and Papa knew. It was time.

We moved to Leicester within a week of arriving in London. I hated it, all of it: the bland food, the water that left a metallic aftertaste in my mouth and the way the relentless wind pressed miserable rain into my bony sides. School was a nightmare, ironic really, given that there was more brown than white at the shitty comprehensive I attended. I sounded different, I pronounced my *t*'s and used archaic words like *thrice*. I adapted soon enough but it was tedious. And the questions, they were the worst, coming at me like hard-hitting hail in a seemingly never-ending storm.

Why did your family move?
Because of the bombs?
Because of the Hindu-Muslim riots?
Will you go back?
Do the mafia run Bombay?
Is it really dangerous?
I didn't know. I didn't want to know. All I knew was Rabbity

was lying on my bed and Caesar was howling beneath it. And I didn't get to wear my mermaid costume at Mona's fancy dress party the following day.

Mama explained when I was a few years older. I didn't ask and I wish she hadn't. I listened in silence, hands curled into tight fists, my knuckles white. She said she'd told me everything, that it was important I know and we should talk about it some more. I said I wanted to be alone and went for a walk. The wind bit at my cheeks as I made sense of her words, and I shivered as the cold truth settled upon me, spreading like an indelible stain over my body. Papa had long left us by then. He walked out on us four years after we moved here.

I hope he burns in shame.

The old, terrible questions are gone. They've been replaced by new, annoying ones. But I've improved. I've learned. To those who ask, I say Papa's dead. To the other question, more frequent than I'd like, I say we moved to Leicester when I was an infant and I've known no other home. It's easier that way.

I moved to London a few years ago, attracted partly by the anonymity it offered. I'm unassuming Nik, uncomplicated and unencumbered by the baggage of the past. I work a four-day week at a property management firm in Putney, I volunteer once a fortnight at the Great Ormond Street Hospital and last month, I joined a running club. No questions asked.

I visit Mama up in Leicester every few months. We're comfortable in our silences, she cooks my favourite pasta, and we watch Hollywood Classics together on DVD. Occasionally she asks me about my job or my friends in London and I tell her what I think she wants to hear.

'Do you ever think about it? Bombay?' she once asked.

I shrugged and began loading the dishwasher.

'Do you remember Rustom's? You loved that store, the old fellow by the till, what was his name, oh I don't know, he used to give you sweets,' she smiled.

'I don't remember.'

'Oh come on, you loved those sweets, Ravalgoan cherry-flavour, wasn't it? You'd beg me to take you …'

'Ma. I said. I don't remember.'

Her face crumpled like the folds of the tea-towel in her hand. I slammed the dishwasher shut.

'Bastard. He's a goddamn bastard,' she hissed, her lips seeping with the rage that had festered for years. She leaned against the kitchen counter, eyes stitched shut, as silent tears slid down her cheeks. I wiped them away, feeling the papery folds of her skin under my palms.

'I'm sorry,' she whispered. 'I'm sorry I allowed him to do this to us.'

She wept. I remained silent. She's not mentioned it again.

I'm home. My hands tremble like leaves in the rain as I empty the carrier bags onto the floor. They form a mosaic at my feet, earthy tones of copper and vermillion, in stark contrast to my pale walls and cream-coloured curtains. I run my fingers through the clothes which are exquisite: silk saris with a delicate dusting of silver dots and embroidered tunics embellished with mirrors. Mama's not worn a sari since we got here and I've never worn one. Sometimes I take the bus to Southall and spend an afternoon walking by the sari shops. I nearly bought one last year, in peacock-green and purple, interwoven with gold threads, but balked at the last minute.

'If you not wanting, why you waste my time,' spat the lady behind the counter. 'Give to me,' she said, snatching the fabric from my hands.

I scuttled out, but for a few fleeting moments I remembered those days when I'd hold on to Mama's sari, tugging at the folds to attract her attention; seeking solace within the pleats to avoid her wrath. And those magical evenings, walking down Marine Drive under the gentle cover of swaying coconut trees. The warmth of the sand between my toes at Chowpatty, sitting on a makeshift bench on the beach, sipping masala milk, Caesar snoozing on my lap, Mama sitting beside me. Innocent memories, now forever tarnished, like a stubborn film of mould formed over a photograph that no amount of effort can ever restore.

I lean against the wall of my poky flat and run my fingers over a crumpled cerise sari. It feels comforting, like balm rubbed onto calloused feet. I rummage around some more and find a pouch filled with earrings. There was a time Mama wouldn't leave the house without them, her dangles and sparkles, but she left them behind. Here, she's worn only the gold dots she had in her ears the night we left. I hold the earrings against my ears, their tinkling reminding me of the faint chiming of the bells as the wind forced its way through open temple windows. Of the priests chanting, the cries of the vegetable vendors on busy market corners, and the cacophony of the tooting yellow-black taxis dotting the city streets. Of old Mrs. Pastakia's off-key singing from the flat below and the sound of Caesar's whines.

The earrings fall to the floor as I cover my ears with my palms.

I cannot bear to have these things in my flat any longer.

I hoist the rucksack onto my back. I've stuffed everything in, down to the last pair of earrings. I walk the short distance to Oxfam, making my way directly to the donations office.

'Oh hey, Nik,' Claire beams. 'Haven't seen you in yonks. More donations?' She walks over as I empty my bag onto the makeshift wooden counter. 'Wow, these are gorgeous,' she breathes, holding a scarf against her neck.

'Thanks.'

'Look at this!' She holds a tunic against her chest and throws the scarf over her head. 'Perfect for dress-up. We'll pull these out just before Halloween. Arabian Nights costumes, eh?' she grins.

A glacial current runs down my spine. 'They're Indian.' My words fall like chips of ice.

'Oops!' she shrugs. She sorts the clothes into little piles.

'I grew up there you know. India. In Mumb…I mean, Bombay.'

'Really?' she smiles. 'Didn't know that. Assumed you were…'

'A-And these clothes, they're old family stuff you know? We didn't bring much actually, we left in…'

'Hmm.' She continues working, head bent low.

I clear my throat. 'It feels unreal now that I think of it,' I continue, the words slipping off my tongue like water off a Teflon pan. 'I mean, from one moment to the next, it's just, everything happened so quickly and…'

'Say, Nik,' she cuts in. 'Sorry, but chat later maybe? I'm in a rush. Gotta get stuff done, leaving early tonight. Got a date,' she winks and turns her attention back to the clothes.

My shoulders droop as I walk to the door.

'See ya later, Nik.'

A jolt of electricity courses through my body. I close my eyes and my hands clench into tight fists. 'It's N-Nikhila,' I say, in a voice I no longer recognise. My name feels foreign in my mouth. 'Nikhila. I'm Nikhila, and I'm from India.'

The words linger for an instant, like a footprint on wet sand, before dissolving into the silence. I know she hasn't heard me.

'Nikhila,' I repeat, louder this time, as I step into the sunshine, feeling the warmth of the syllables on my tongue. 'Nik-hil-a.'

It is enough for today.

Author's Note: The Bombay bombings were a series of 12 bomb explosions that took place in Bombay on 12th March 1993. The single-day attacks, perpetuated by the Bombay mafia resulted in over 250 fatalities and left nearly 800 injured.
This is a work of fiction.

THE INVENTORY

Deblina Chakrabarty

'The blue floral dinner set, the one with the gravy bowl. You take that. That's English anyway so it will be suitable over there. Ma never quite knew what to do with that gravy bowl. I remember she used to put the mango chutney in that.'

Sujata Di sat across me scribbling away. A stubborn ballpoint pen scratched away at the flimsy ruled-pad under her purposeful grip. She looked like a government official, making decisive notes that determine pensions, provident funds, land allocations and such. I wanted to tell her that the gravy bowl was as obscure in London as it was here, in my mother's house. No one had gravy anymore, except with soggy Sunday roasts in their local pubs. And that came pre-slopped, on top of the depressingly cratered Yorkshire puddings, not served daintily alongside in a blue floral patterned bone china gravy bowl. But I said nothing. It would probably be interpreted as condescension. Everything about my life in London was a direct affront to my sister who had never travelled abroad.

It seemed surreal – us sisters sitting calmly at my mother's worn dining table, half-drunk cups of lukewarm tea flanking us like it was any ordinary weekday mid-morning. The only difference was the silence in the kitchen. If my mother had been there, there would've been the preparatory hisses and sizzles of lunch-making with an errant sneeze or two if the chili was being tempered along with the mustard seeds.

Instead we sat running through Ma's things, trying to make sense of her life, packing it away, absorbing it, preserving it, disposing of it. At that moment I wished I was rich, in an English sort of way. Like Arup's legal clients back home. Those people with trusts and estates. So many old people lived alone and died with their lives invisibly arranged and artfully disposed of in their death. Presumably by English gentlemen with pocket squares and an ampersand in between their names.

'How about Baba's armchair?' I ventured.

I toyed with the idea of shipping it back to London. The old planter's chair still bore clumsy etchings of my school pencils and was a totem pole of all things home. It carried the fading memories of my father's afternoon naps, the Statesman[1] spread-eagled on his chest. It had been my favourite place to sit and read in between meals when I came to visit Ma every year, picking out increasingly moth-eaten copies of Sujata Di's *Tess of D'Urberville* or *Mill on the Floss*. I always wondered why she hadn't taken her books to her own house which was twenty minutes away and cleaned them up, given them a better life so to speak. It's almost as if she had left a part of her old self here in our mother's house, one she couldn't bear to reclaim.

'Oh don't worry I can take that. It will be a nice addition to the guesthouse veranda. These visitors have become so picky nowadays. Ooff, everything needs to be *vintage* and *boutique*. Calcutta is not Sabyasachi's designer showroom, but who's to tell

---

1 Daily newspaper in Kolkata, once the leading daily of its time

them that! Here everything is dusty and noisy and things get corroded just standing on four stationary legs. Romance of the monsoons my foot! Come see us after the romance is ended!'

I cringed at the thought of our chair being a careless prop in Di's flailing guesthouse business. Sudeep Da's crumbling family home had once been a wild, majestic beauty up near Park Circus when I was a child and Di newly married into a cultural rarity – a Bengali business family. But forty years and many wrong turns later, all that remained was a mildewed cracked edifice that badly needed repairs, overgrown with weeds and encroached by squatters in the backyard. Despite this, it tried to keep the entire family afloat by pretending to be a *Heritage Bed & Breakfast In The Heart of Old Calcutta.*

But it made sense I suppose. How would I explain this weather-beaten mahogany anomaly to my Scandinavian sofas and Italian glass tables back home? I was pretty sure they wouldn't make it feel welcome. It would stick out uncertainly and Arup would knock his stiffening knees against it as he rushed to work. I would begin by defending it loyally, sitting on it for my morning tea, always slightly amazed at how much lower it suddenly felt and how much harder it was to hoist myself out of it. It would be too big for the guest rooms. So one Saturday when the handyman came in to rearrange the paintings and fix the panel in the kitchen cabinet, he would matter-of-factly also dismantle the chair and put it in the garage along with Other Things I Love Too Much To Throw But Don't Know How To Use.

'Is Arup coming for the *Shraadh*[2] at least?' Di sprung that question at me like the next item of Ma's things, sweeping me from my London house back into Ma's eerily empty flat.

---

2 Funeral in Bengali

'Erm, of course he is. He was going to come last week but I thought, we all thought, she was getting better, so I told him to wrap work up and come over at the weekend, and then she …'

'…and then she didn't.' Di's staccato landed like a quiet slap, forcing us to face the reality of the moment beyond crockery and furniture. 'Too bad her *favourite* son-in-law wasn't here to see her one last time.'

'Di really? Why now? What is the point even? Ma isn't here, you know, to have a go at.' A headache began to creep up my temples.

'Why? What am I saying that's not true? It was always Arup, the successful son-in-law. And Shohini the career woman. Her successful children. Bringing English jams and biscuits twice a year. Getting the bathroom renovated. Giving her that ridiculous video phone she could never use. Not once! Sashaying in and out twice a year like beauty contestants. But where were you for the doctors' visits? Do you know how long the waiting is, even when we had appointments? Do you know how impossible it is to park in peak traffic and then escort a frail old person from the car to the clinic? Do you have any idea how many forms need to be filled for each insurance claim?'

Di's staccato rose to a crescendo through this tirade. There was nothing new or untrue in anything she said so why interject? If this was the only way she could express her grief at Ma's passing, then that's what she needed to do. At least she had found some outlet, while I lay suspended in the soundless miasma of Ma's absence.

After the involuntary heave of tears at Ma's nose being stuffed with cotton wool and her being carried out of the house on a stretcher, all I had experienced was the stress of endless administrative activities and the eerie orderly silence of the house around us. How quickly and casually our neighbours and relatives had begun referring to Ma as 'the body'. While she was still lying there! All those things which had been *her* things became *things* within an hour, and now lay lifeless, agape, awaiting a verdict on their posthumous fate. And here stood Di and I, the reluctant executioners, trying to find our mother, our sisterly camaraderie (did we ever have it?), a way forward, amidst the debris of our childhood.

'*Cha khabey*? I'll make us both another cup,' I offered to defuse the mood and try and compensate for a painkiller. This headache looked like it was going to be staying a while. Ma's kitchen was from another century. It had nothing in common with the sleek lines of my eat-in version back home. There were no appliances, minimal utensils (*utensils*, not kitchenware, I silently laughed to myself) and everything had that oily sheen that was inescapable in the absence of electric chimneys and the ubiquity of mustard-oil infused curries. And yet the sublime simple flavours of her mixed vegetable *shukto,* or her dried-lentil *dhokar dalna* had proved un-duplicable back in London. I had tried in the early days with naïve enthusiasm and then given up. You can't have everything everywhere all the time I had reasoned.

'You know Di, despite what Ma used to say, I think you should have her jewellery. All of it.'

We had hesitantly made our way to Ma's bedroom, both of us sitting gingerly on the window ledge – anywhere but the bed – in silent synchronicity. Ma's Godrej cupboard stood ajar as Di bypassed the jewellery box to look through the myriad other silver tins and carved wooden boxes stuffed with keys, papers, stray bangles, a tarnished miniature Lakshmi statuette, detritus of a lived life.

'Why? Please *ei shob koro na*. I don't want any ugliness later. Especially over jewellery, like those greedy Marwaris families, always in the newspapers for property disputes.'

She didn't even look at me while she went through all the yellowing papers, trying not to tear them along their ancient folds. I still remembered Di on her wedding day, outside of the square sepia-tinted photos lying compressed in those albums in the living room. On her, the gold had looked iridescent, heavy like those temple jewels on goddesses as she sat at the altar, a vision in red and white. How handsome Sudeep Da had been back then. Slightly cocky in that delightful way you can afford to be when you're young, wealthy and the only son of a well-to-do family in socialist Bengal. In my memory I was a gangly pre-teen in an organza saree wrapped awkwardly around me as I scampered around, evading any wedding duty and revelling in the beauty of Di's magnificent white new mansion, with its giant trees in the courtyard and a black and white chequered marble porch. Marble, what luxury, Ma had whispered to Baba on the night of Sudeep Da's *ashirbad*[3].

'Why would she keep this? I don't understand,' Di was muttering to herself, brows scrunched up as she stumbled back to sit on the bed.

'What is it?' I was worried now. Very few things managed to frazzle Di. This must be serious.

'A poem. Dr. Sarkar had written to me.'

'Tridib Da? From Dover Lane? *Your* Tridib?'

Faint memories came trickling back. He had been a young

---

3 Bengali version of engagement which happens individually and separately for bride and groom with each receiving gifts and blessings from friends and relatives.

GP in the neighbourhood. Ma Baba had called him when Di had had one of her seizures, except that this one had been much longer than usual. And our regular doctor had been away on holiday. It struck me how completely I had forgotten about Tridib Sarkar, given how much of a presence he – or his name – had been that one summer in our house when I was ten. Was this what the shrinks mean by repressed memory? But why would I need to repress this? It wasn't even my memory, it was Di's.

'Chhee Tumpa, he's married, what are you thinking,' Ma's admonitory tone was in strange contrast to her use of Di's *daak naam*[4]. The hushed tone might have been for my benefit but I was at the age where I had learned the advantages of feigned sleep. I hadn't seen what the big deal was, why Ma and Baba were so grim and disapproving. He wasn't so old. And he was so handsome with wavy black hair and aquiline features, like a prince from those comic books I used to read back then. And he had the most wonderful deep voice that I could hear on the veranda when he sat with a cup of tea made by Di as she adoringly basked in his maturity, his erudition, his kindness.

But then one day he was gone. And no one ever mentioned him in front of me again. Di had a few seizures in quick succession, usually on the back of a muffled heated argument with Ma behind closed doors. Baba usually stayed out of it. He barely spoke to Di in those days. Until he came home one day with Sudeep Da's bio. And then the wedding juggernaut pushed everything else out of sight.

'Where did she find it? I thought I had lost it. Why did she

---

4 Pet name. Every Bengali has a pet name that's completely disconnected from their real/formal name i.e. it's not an abbreviation.

even keep it?' Di was still muttering, her face a disapproving frown eerily reminiscent of Ma, and her voice unfamiliarly soft in its contours, bringing back memories of a young Di from a long time ago.

'Maybe she felt bad for both of you. Maybe she was sorry,' I ventured tentatively. It was the closest I could go near the emotional and financial decline her years with Sudeep had been.

'Sorry? For what? It was nonsense. Who writes a poem to another girl when he's already married? Sudeep would never do that.' Di's censure carried the whiff of a broken heart from a long time ago. I didn't want to tell her that Sudeep wouldn't – couldn't – write a poem if his life was under jeopardy. His passions were a combination of pecuniary gains and hypochondriac aches, and since he had neither, conversations – and I imagine life – with him was hostile, exhausting and dull all at once.

I watched Di fold the paper into its tiny square and stuff it into her purse with her mobile and keys. I was glad she had found it.

You can't have everything everywhere all the time, but you can have some things, sometimes, just for yourself.

'Shohini listen, this isn't going to work. Please just tell me all the things you want. Please don't do this 'Di you take everything' nonsense. I know you and Arup are very rich in England but don't shove that in my face. Not with Ma's things.'

'But I'm taking the albums, the dinner set, Ma's wedding saree, those silver glasses...'

'And what about the other sarees, the old copper cooking pots, the pickle jars, the mirrored cabinet? You're not even taking any

76

of the bed linen. Am I supposed to throw perfectly new things away?'

The exhaustion of the day had added shrillness to her usual stridency. I wondered what we'd do after the business of settling Ma's house was done. Would we still see each other twice a year, unbound by the umbilical cord Ma formed between us? She couldn't travel to London. She didn't have the money or the will. Would I come back more often? To stay here? Alone? That could be a possibility couldn't it?

'Di, I told you our beds have fitted sheets and duvets. We don't use flat sheets and bed covers. It's just … it's just different there. And anyway why are we in a hurry to get rid of everything? I mean like furniture and linen can still be used…for the house, right?'

'What do you mean? We have to sell the house. You surely understood that?'

The words sank like fresh snow into my mind, settling softly, yet sinking deep. Of course I should have seen that was a real possibility. Empty flats in decrepit buildings aren't considered assets in Calcutta the way they are in London. The rental market is either non-existent or an eviction nightmare skewed in the tenants' favour. And I couldn't imagine strangers living in Ma's house either. Di had her crumbling guesthouse and Sudeep. Her daughter Piu was working in Bangalore, supervisor at one of those BPOs, not eager to return to Calcutta which she found depressing and had run from as fast as she could.

And me?

Arup and I had casually lobbed the D-word a few times these past years. After Sayon left home for university, the space in between us was too large to be ignored. I had resorted to Gü chocolate pots and reruns of Downton Abbey in the TV room. Arup probably resorted to the comforting admirations of his revolving door of young female interns and colleagues. I doubt philandering was our original problem. It would've easier if it had been. I hadn't had the heart or words to tell Ma anything. And what would I have told her? That we were disenchanted with each other? We had lost the connection? I was acutely aware of how First World and self-indulgent these words sounded. They didn't befit a hard-working couple who had had the opportunity to migrate and then had a series of lucky breaks at the right time that gave them both their own careers along with a beautiful baby boy.

'What if…if we need it some day?' I stuttered to Di. There was no point telling her about Arup and me right now. We weren't close that way anyway.

'Need it some day? We need it today, my dear. Do you think Ma's treatments came for free?' Di's voice had begun to rise again, dark circles appearing around her eyes as the day receded outside the window around us.

'There is no need to be condescending, Di. I consistently sent money. And Ma said her savings and insurance covered most of it.'

'That's what she told you because she didn't want to bother you. And she didn't know the details either. Most of her savings were in fixed deposits. The insurance took ages to recoup and we only got partial amounts back. Those LIC[5] guys are crooks. You should see the way Sudeep had to run around to their Esplanade office, days on end, in this summer heat. We had to take out loans to

---

5 Life Insurance Company of India; the biggest state-owned insurance company in India

tide us over. We aren't rich like you and Arup. But we were here.'

The word 'loan' snuck in between the accusatory tirade was the Trojan army she hoped I wouldn't spot. Ma and Baba had abhorred debt of any kind. They had even bought their flat with savings and their modest inheritances. But Sudeep was familiar with debt. A bit too familiar from what I had heard in whispers at family gatherings. I was too tired to ask her why we couldn't break the fixed deposits and repay the loans instead of selling the flat. I knew she needed any money she could get. It would buy her some breathing room, some autonomy no matter how temporary, in her marriage. There is nothing worse than a proud woman with no income of her own. It can destroy you.

And what would I have told her to stop her anyway? Can we please keep the house until I figure out if Arup and I can salvage our marriage? Until we figure out if we want to do so? I may still never be able to move back and live here. I have work and my son in London. But I like the *idea* of having my mother's house ready and waiting for me whenever I might want to return?

My headache was killing me. I hoped a splash of water on my face and neck would help until I could get to a painkiller. I couldn't imagine the thought of sleeping through it. The bathroom shelf was bare. A solitary bottle of Ponds talcum powder and Keo Karpin hair oil sat stolidly on their perch. Next to it was the shallow bowl with my mother's dentures. The full set of upper and lower jaw teeth, stained brown with age, food, paan[6]. I had always thought the slight aloofness and detachment of these teeth from her gums added a sweetness to her smile that real teeth couldn't provide. Even the brown stains reminded me of liquid jaggery drizzled over winter desserts. But

---

6 Betel leaf, usually chewed after meals as a digestive

she had always used her teeth as a cautionary tale for us growing up. 'If you don't brush thrice a day you will get pyorrhoea and all your teeth will fall out,' and we would run sleepily to the bathroom to chew on our toothbrushes. She had been a rare victim of extreme periodontitis in her late twenties and lack of timely intervention had led to her losing all her teeth by the time she was thirty.

I had been born when Ma was thirty-two – two years after her teeth had fallen out. I had learnt first-hand how hard it can be to sustain love and attraction in a marriage. I imagined being thirty and toothless with Arup. I wondered what he would have done. These days he discreetly eyed my Gü-thickened waist which only made my midnight raids more frequent. I remember trying to ask Ma how it had been with Baba after the teeth fell out. She pretended not to understand my question. But secretly I had felt overjoyed. I was a love-child in the true sense of the word. Despite this damning cosmetic calamity, Ma and Baba had found enough man-woman love between them to have me, ten years after Di. A 'happy accident' as we call them in India.

I knew what I had to take back with me to London. Ma's teeth were a triumph; a testimony of hope and love from simpler times. It was the closest I could get to having her wide, generous smile with me forever, urging me to forge ahead, despite everything. Reminding me to hold on to what I had without ruing what I had lost. I didn't think Di would care or approve so I quietly slipped them into the battered tin recently emptied of Tridib's poem. It seemed a fitting abode.

I hadn't seen that smile – one of helplessness and relief – on Di's face for a long time but it was there when I came out of the bathroom and told her, 'It's OK, Di, you can sell the flat if you need to. I trust you to do what's best. Just tell me what you need from me. I've taken what I want of Ma's.'

CIVIL LINES

One Man's Chronicle of Partition

Kavita A. Jindal

[i]

'Rice fields are rice fields wherever they are.'
My youngest sister says this to console me.
'Look how green the fields gleam
under the noon sun here in Karnal,
just like in Sheikhupura.
The cows chew the cud the same.
The milk is good, *na*?'

Lassi here does *not* taste the same.
Pulao does *not* taste the same.
It should, I know, it should be delicious,
but my tongue has forgotten flavour.
We are the lucky ones, the survivors.

God has been good to us. We can regain
in part, our material losses.

I will never again see the lamp-post at the end of
my street. The one I sulked under my whole youth.
Where I sat alone to dream and to read
my English books in peace. I will never again show
my sons the land tilled by their forefathers; the two
white houses of their childhood; quite the grandest
homes in town.

'Remove your cloak of sorrow,' my sister says.
'Life is yours to enjoy.' I have to admit my father
has taken the blow better than me. *We will build again.*
He constructs new houses on empty plots of land.
But my home is left behind. Here does not suffice.
Not Karnal, not Delhi, not Bombay, nothing has the same
fragrance, nothing tastes the same. Life has no flavour.

[ii]

I had a younger brother who was a simpleton,
not right in the head. Didn't understand the world,
was difficult to control. He could be dangerous,
unwitting. Once he dropped my baby daughter
from the roof terrace like she was a toy.
Miraculously, she was unhurt.

That evening of genocide in late August 1947
we hid him with us in the fields. We crouched into
new shoots hardly daring to breathe, praying that
the Balochi soldiers (or mob, whatever you want to call
the vigilantes, armies, and marauding bands of that time)
would not discover us.

My brother couldn't stay quiet.
He didn't understand. We pulled
him down as he stood up in the dusk.
We pinned his legs and arms.
He shouted, he babbled. I whispered:
'Shh. Shh. We'll all be killed.

Don't you hear them baying for blood?'
Some of them our people, our neighbours,
intent on spilling blood.
'Why-y? Why-y?' my brother called out
like children do, and we couldn't quiet him.
I risked a glance above the green stalks.

A small gang, maybe eight men
approached us, palms cupped to ears,
listening on the wind to his whimpers.
Stamping the crop as they advanced.
We left him. My father and I.
We left my brother.

We slithered away on our chests, then crawled
on hands and knees in the direction of a refugee camp.

Surely from there they would take us to this invisible
"border", that we needed to find, get beyond,
be on the other side of a line of demarcation
freshly drawn on British paper.

Clothes in shreds, mud in our mouths
we tried to cross to what had become
another country. It would be our "nation".
But in my mouth there was only the taste of mud.
The mud of my fields. The imagined blood
of my brother. We don't know what happened to him.

[iii]

The women and children were summering in Simla.
A neighbour there heard the news first.
One white bungalow burned down.
The other commandeered.
(Later, it became the local jail!)

Everything in the houses taken. 'All gone, empty,'
the neighbour said. Though how could he know?
He read my wife the day's gazette. '10,000 non-Muslim
civilians murdered. In one evening.' Some were listed.
My father's name and mine. Recorded under 'Killed'.

Almost a month later in Simla
my wife opened the door to me.
I knew what it was to come back from the dead.
I saw it in her eyes.
Was I just an emaciated ghost?

Were we naïve to believe, even ten days past Partition
that our town wouldn't turn on us? That the flames
that licked at all hearts and all doors that month
would spare us? I didn't think everything would be
consumed in the name of Freedom. In 1947 was
everyone else insane or were we?

Insane to believe we would be secure in
our courtyard of privilege, wearing the turbans
of our faith? Our ancestors had settled to farm
and prosper. I had even counted back seven generations
on the land, and seven generations ago
we were Hindu before we became Sikh.

How many faiths and saints had this fertile soil produced?
How many kings and conquerors had renamed the place?
We lived among believers who believed in numerous ways.
A thousand ways to be Hindu. A hundred ways to follow Islam.
Discreet believers of other sects, not fitting in with the diktats
of temple, mosque, gurudwara, church.

They all belonged in our town. We had myriad ways to
pray and celebrate. Could I have known that we had myriad
ways of viciousness and loathing simmering within us?
That we were susceptible to politics, our leaders' divisions,
armies rising to respond to a call for the Sikhs who
stayed put on their estates to be driven out.

The night of the mob there was one man
who remained a beacon of humanity.
To him we owe the chance of our new beginnings.
'Bhagoo Nai', our family barber, slipped into our house
minutes ahead of the massacre-pack.

'Flee. Now. Hide somewhere,' he begged.
Chittian kothiyan wale sardar will be attacked first.
He'd heard this at the meeting as the soldiers prepared.
Bhagoo put loyalty and humanity first.
He was a *musalman* who risked himself, placing

his real conscience ahead of tribesmanship.
He was the reason we chose not to surrender
to hatred. No matter what we heard and saw
of what they did; and what we did; all those horrors
each side had perpetrated; no matter how many

wars are whipped up between old and new country,
I cannot be harsh with others, on the basis of
religion alone. And, no matter your chiding,
I can't help but mourn my real home
where I won't be able to return.

* *Chittian kothiyan wale sardar*: the Sikhs of the white houses
* *musalman*: Muslim

THIS CAN BE MINE

Mona Dash

The 394 arrives and Sonal files in with the others. The white people – she calls them *gore log* – always seem calm. They don't push. They stand silently, waiting for those on the bus to step down, then the driver waits for everyone to board. Once on, people give others space, even if the bus is full, and try to keep their hands and legs to themselves. Back home in Baroda, the buses often pull away, loaded beyond capacity, while people are still trying to get on. On board, they jostle elbows, bags and umbrellas, sweating from the heat. Now, she stares, as she always does, at the *gore log's* clothes. Today, most are wearing shorts or dresses, sandals instead of the high boots she had seen when she first arrived in this country a few months ago. She shivers in spite of the sun and pulls her jacket closer. A navy jacket, one of her first purchases, bought with her own money, fourteen pounds earned after two hours of cleaning. She had seen it in the window of the Cancer Research shop. She hadn't realised the clothes were second-hand until later, when the shop assistant asked her to try it, and she, thinking it was too tight, asked for a bigger size.

'There is no other size,' the old lady smiled, her white, curled hair marvellously kept, 'We can only offer what is donated.'

Sonal bought it, the navy jacket with large grey buttons that fits tight on her waist and flares around her like a dress. Later, she found a very crumpled Sainsbury's bill dated 23rd April 2015 in a pocket. For some reason, she kept it, as if it was hers, as if she had worn that jacket, two years ago, gone into Sainsbury's on the High Street and bought a bottle of red wine and pitted green olives with garlic for a whole ten pounds.

Sonal finds a seat, looks out of the window and counts the stops. She must get off at Orpington High street, turn left at the post office, walk down the road until she comes to an old fashioned street lamp, look towards the right and she will see an alley, go down the alley, and on her right she'll see a house with a blue door and steps leading up to it. On the phone, Rina Patel, had been helpful and given her detailed directions. Premila usually cooks for her but she's away in India for a month and has distributed her jobs between Sonal and the other girls.

Premila, or Premila *behn* as they addressed her, as you should, out of respect, is an institution. Back home in Gujarat everyone knew that once you reached London and needed work, you got in touch with Premila *behn*. She found cooking, cleaning and babysitting jobs for you. While the *desis* can find everything they want in the London stores, even Indian spices and vegetables, where can they find the cooks and cleaners that they are used to? Premila *behn* often joked about that. The other girls spoke of her income in whispers, almost two thousand pounds every month, they thought. She carried wads of cash in her bag, they said. She didn't ask for commissions, her reward was the wide network she established. She boasted she could find girls in places like Barnet and Chiswick even though she herself lived in Mottingham.

As always, she had asked Kuresh for directions to Rina Patel's house. He checked Google maps and grunted the instructions.

'It's close enough to the high street. Walk down Leyton Street, and then there's a small lane on the left and you walk on it until…'

'The woman said there's an old-fashioned street lamp. What did she mean?'

He said nothing. There is so much he still doesn't know about this country even though he has been here for five years whereas she, after six months, feels she has a sense of the place.

'Is it one of those you know, the old type, the beautiful lantern-like lamps, not the modern streetlight?'

'Nothing in this country is modern,' he'd replied, turning his attention to the pile of *chapattis* and curry and eating rapidly.

The street light is indeed beautiful. An octagonal lamp hangs on one end of a wrought iron bar with circles and rectangles swirling on the bronze pole. At the top, there is an etching of what looks like a small child. She wonders how old the lamp is, why it has been placed here.

The instructions are perfect. Soon, she climbs the five steps to the blue door and knocks. The door is opened by a woman, almost as slim as her. She's wearing a white lace top and those ripped jeans Sonal hasn't dared try. The rips show her golden brown thighs and knees. Sonal notices the large shiny watch on her wrist. Like an actress in a movie, she thinks.

'Sonal? Hello! I'm Rina Patel. We spoke. Come in, come in.'

The kitchen is a wide room, a black granite counter in the middle, a marble dining table in the corner. A massive vase of large pink blooms stands in the centre of the table. Sonal catches their fragrance but doesn't know what the flowers are. She hears music. It's not Hindi and she can't make out the English words.

'So what can you cook, Sonal?' the lady asks with a smile. Her hair falls straight on her shoulders.

'Anything you ask for.'

'Premila *behn* normally makes *parathas,* stuffed *parathas,* also *dhoklas.*'

'I can make all of that. Non-veg also. Fish, chicken…anything.' Show a willingness to work, Premila *behn* advised them all.

'That's great. So when did you come to England?'

'Since a long time.'

'Oh, OK. I thought Premila *behn* said you are new.'

That was the problem with Premila *behn*. You never knew whom she told what. She'd instructed her girls to say they'd been in the country a while to reassure families that they knew how everything worked, but she's told the family Sonal's a recent arrival.

'No, I have been here. I can do all work, hoover, dish washer, washing machine. I know all.'

'That's good but I just need some cooking done today. Didn't she tell you that?' The lady looks worried.

'Yes I can, no problem. Whatever she was doing, I can do.'

The lady's request is simple. Some *dhoklas* and some *parathas.* Sonal sets about mixing the semolina with flour. The lady says she doesn't have a *dhokla* container and keeps forgetting to buy one so Premila *behn* sets up a contraption for steaming.

'I know how to do that too,' Sonal says.

She fills a pan with water, places a couple of spoons in it and gently sits the bowl with the *dhokla* mix on the spoons. The mix will cook in the steam. She will then cut the fluffy *dhoklas* into squares and flavour them with mustard seeds and coriander leaves. She makes *parathas* and pads them with potatoes. She calls out when she's done and the lady, she must address her as Rina *behn*, appears from upstairs.

"You are very quick! Premila *behn* takes longer. My husband really likes these,' she says, gesturing at the pile of food now laid out on trays, and then towards the living room.

Sonal notices photos on the mantelpiece. A family photo, the husband smiling, Rina *behn* in a strappy dress, shoulders shining, face turned towards him, her arms around the two children. That's when she realises the husband is a *gora*, and the children look so different from Indian children. The boy has blue eyes in his light brown face. The girl has very fair skin and dark hair. She hears them outside. Through the kitchen window she sees them on the trampoline jumping up and down, up and down.

'He's not Indian,' she blurts. She is staring at the photo. She's surprised that she's inside the house of a foreigner, as they call them in India.

'No, he's not, but he loves Indian food and yet *parathas* take so much time…you know,' Rina *behn* explains.

That's not what Sonal wants to know. She wants to know how it happened, where she met him, how they got married. But Rina *behn* asks if she can come once a week, every week, for three hours. If she finishes the cooking she can do some ironing perhaps?

Sonal agrees. Getting regular jobs is her priority. The type of work is secondary. Babysitting the most prized, followed by cooking, and then cleaning. She takes the cash, seven pounds an hour, fourteen pounds in total. After some more experience, she can ask for eight pounds an hour. She races back to the High Street and waits for another bus to go to Sidcup for her second job of her day.

The next week, Rina *behn* has a slightly different request. 'Can you make cauliflower curry?'

Sonal cuts cauliflowers into small florets and fries them with potatoes and onions. Cumin seeds nestle in the florets.

Later Rina *behn* looks a bit disappointed 'Is that how you cook cauliflower? We normally break the florets in bigger chunks, we fry them, then stir a thick gravy...I just can't make it as well as my mum.' Her face falls.

Sonal is annoyed. 'But, why didn't you tell me what you wanted? I can make what you want. Do you want me to make it again?'

'Oh, don't worry. It's all right!'

It rankles her however. She is a good cook, she knows. She could have made this curry whatever way was required.

'Which part of India are you from?' Sonal asks.

'Calcutta. I am a Bengali. And you? You are from Gujarat, isn't it?'

'Yes.' And in spite of herself she asks, 'How did you meet your husband?'

'I came here to study. I met Paul for the first time in a café.' Her voice rises, her face lights in animation. Sonal imagines them, holding hands, kissing. One of the framed wedding pictures sits on the mantelpiece, Rina *behn*'s brown shoulders gleaming against white lace. Sonal feels jealous. She thinks of Kuresh and with a sigh turns away.

'And you, Sonal, how did you meet your husband?' Rina *behn* really seems a friendly person. None of her other customers have asked her this.

'A proposal came. My parents accepted.' She had seen Kuresh only on their wedding day. She remembers his hasty fingers in the night, trying to unravel her saree.

'Your parents must miss you then. You are so far away. Do you go back to India often?'

Everyone was happy that the proposal was for a boy living in London. No one in her family had ever gone abroad.

'I may go next year,' she replies. They need to sort their visas, save some more money. Next year will be difficult, she knows.

The next weekend, Rina *behn* has much more for Sonal to do. She's invited ten families for dinner and Sonal must prepare as much as she can before the guests arrive. But she was late for her first job, then the bus was late too, and here she is two hours late.

And her period is late too. Very late. She hasn't told Kuresh yet. She knows he won't be happy.

Rina *behn* is standing in the kitchen looking worried. 'People will be arriving soon. How long will it take, do you think?'

'Don't worry, I will be quick.' Sonal is already kneading the dough for *parathas*. She has to make fifty. Rina *behn* has prepared the chicken and lamb. They hear the doorbell and Rina *behn* rushes out of the kitchen, her grey dress all softness and ruffles. Sonal hears the hellos, the kisses in the air, the laughter. She turns her head to watch the guests coming in. They look like the box of chocolates Kuresh had given her at the airport. A box of Lindor, some black, white and brown. The children come in quietly and

94

politely, but once in the garden all that changes. They shout, they jump up and down on the trampoline. A few try somersaults. One of them trips, falls and cries.

She rolls the dough into balls and counts them. The pile keeps growing, as she rolls and fries, rolls and fries. A woman comes in, giggling.

'Where can I get some water?' she asks, trying to compose herself. She wears a black, sleeveless dress, her arms white but her skin is dry. A man follows. He's laughing too.

'You haven't listened to all of it.' He grabs her arm.

She laughs louder and falls back into him. He cups her face and kisses her, then looks up and smiles at Sonal.

'Hi,' he says.

She doesn't reciprocate. She continues cooking. The *gore log* can't be trusted. You never know what they will do next. How can they kiss standing close to someone they don't even know?

That evening, back home, she faces Kuresh. 'Lipkiss,' she says.

He stares at her uncomprehending. Then laughs. 'Where did you learn that? It's not night yet!'

She retreats to the kitchen and starts cooking. It's been two weeks and she hasn't told him. She's been brave and bought a pregnancy test from Superdrug and watched two lines turn dark pink. They haven't even been married a year. They haven't talked about babies. It must be some mistake with the dates, with the protection he should have used, though he will blame her, she knows. She is here on a student visa, except that she hasn't completed the course. Kuresh is also on a student visa but instead of studying, he's working in his uncle's shops. The uncle and aunt have no children which is why they arranged for Kuresh to come here. One day, when his uncle can no longer work,

95

Kuresh will take over the shop. The government has changed the rules, their uncle explained, and it has become difficult to obtain permanent residency in the UK. Before you could apply for citizenship after five years but not now. In his uncle's days, there wasn't even a citizenship test to pass. Until he works out a plan, they have to be careful. They can never leave the country. They must hide in the crevices, unseen and unregistered by anyone.

How can they bring a baby into the world? Sonal asks herself.

The next week, when she arrives at Rina *behn*'s house, she finds the kitchen is a mess. She wipes the oil spattered on the counter, then notices thick blobs on the extractor unit waiting to land on the hob. She wets a sponge and starts to scrape it off.

'The cleaner hasn't come. Again,' Rina *behn* says.

'How often does she come?'

'She's meant to come once a week, but she rarely does…'

'Is she a *gori*?' Sonal blurts out.

'She is from Romania. Eastern Europe,' Rina *behn* says, as if in explanation.

Sonal offers to clean. 'These *gore log* can't be trusted,' she says. Rina *behn* doesn't smile. Of course, her husband is one of them, but nor does she defend them.

The hoover is massive. Sonal drags it upstairs, up the steps. The extra work means the envelope with the pound notes in her cupboard will fill up a little bit faster. She worries about lifting heavy things with a baby growing inside her.

The next week, she makes an excuse not to hoover, saying that her back hurts. She needs to make excuses for three more weeks. Then she will be twelve weeks and can tell everyone. That's what they believe. You don't share good news before the twelfth week. She feels bad lying.

But Rina *behn* guesses. The next week, when Sonal says she has back ache and can't take the hoover up the stairs, she asks gently, 'I hope you are looking after yourself? Eating well? Have you had your lunch?'

She hasn't. All she's eaten is a bar of chocolate. She nods.

She told Kuresh a few days ago. He was quiet for a while.

'It's all right,' he said finally when he came to bed. 'In this country, we needn't worry. The medical care is free. The school is free. We earn enough for food. Prem *Chacha* has added our names as dependents with the GP, and no questions were asked. Why should they ask now? There is nothing to worry about.'

She was relieved. That night she'd slept well.

The bus journeys take so long. Waiting at the bus stop, sometimes changing two or three times to get to one house. She looks at the babies in their prams. Tucked in, comfortable. When she goes to Tesco to buy *masoor* dal, she runs her fingers over baby clothes.

It's the next morning, when she's ready to leave, that she feels the pain. At first it's a slow ache in her stomach. Then she's pushing out lumpy masses. She wants to hold on to it and re-shape the blood into what it was meant to be. She knows enough to understand. Her voice cracks when she shouts to Kuresh.

'It's all those jobs you do,' he says. 'I told you to stop it, didn't I? But you wanted your own money.'

He calls for a cab and they go to the hospital. The procedure is quicker than she expects.

'Would you like to have a photo of the scan?' the nurse asks.

Kuresh says, 'It's not necessary,' but she is nodding her head and the nurse has noticed.

'There you go, just a little memento. You will be fine soon, dear. Put your feet up for a few days.'

Sonal wants to tell the nurse that back home they don't make a big deal of these things. The child who doesn't want to come is removed and forgotten. That's all there is to it. To wrap it, give it a burial and attach a thousand dreams to it is a fad of the *gore log*.

Her mother tells her to drink *neem* juice every day to clean her insides and to try again in a few weeks. Her parents don't know they don't want a baby now. They are saving, they are trying to build themselves a future. Her parents don't understand that she doesn't want to mourn for what came, unasked. Everyone wants to replace it, like a new TV.

She doesn't sleep much. She imagines a pain where they scraped away at her, but there is nothing. She has some more paracetamol and when she wakes, she sees Kuresh is getting ready for work.

'Can you take the day off?'

'Why? You're feeling better, aren't you? It's month end. I have to help Prem *Chacha* with the books.'

She nods. She isn't in pain, not really. She wouldn't even have known, everything was so quick. She hasn't opened the envelope with the photo of the scan. It sits in her bag.

She goes back to work after three days. Rina *behn* says she needn't hoover today.

'I can now,' she says, dragging the hoover up the stairs. 'I had a miscarriage.'

98

'Sorry…what did you say?' Rina *behn* comes rushing upstairs. 'Sonal, are you all right? What happened? Should you be working?'

'Yes. I am fine.'

She wants to say she has a photo of the baby, the baby she hadn't planned to have, but who came to her uninvited. She wants to show Rina *behn* the photo. She wants to sit down on the landing, right now, and weep on Rina *behn's* soft cream carpets. She fiddles with the plug of the hoover instead.

Rina *behn's* face crumples into sadness. 'Oh Sonal, I am sorry,' she says. 'It happened to one of my friends last year. She was very upset…we consoled her… but she is seven months pregnant now!' She stands awkwardly next to Sonal and reaches a hand out, resting it on Sonal's arm.

'It happens sometimes,' Sonal shrugs.

In her world it's not meant to matter. Rina *behn*, she thinks, in your world you can mourn then celebrate the next time, clinking glasses of wine.

'It will be fine. Don't worry,' Rina *behn* continues. 'I am going to Eastham. I need to go to the temple. My mother made a promise, you know, like a *mannat*? My son was unwell, so she promised that when he is better, I will offer a *puja* in the temple.' Rina *behn* rolls her eyes in disbelief. 'Would you like to come with me?'

Sonal agrees. She intended to go to the temple some time and now she can travel comfortably in the car.

The kids stay with the husband with his white skin, blue eyes, dark brown hair. Sonal likes the different colours of the *gore log's* eyes and hair. She's never spoken to him but she likes it when he smiles at her, when he says hello. He walks to the door with them and gives Rina *behn* a hug, then stands and waves as Rina *behn* pulls out of the driveway. She drives fast, often muttering or swearing. Sometimes she lifts her hand and waves a thank you. This is how it is done in this country.

Eastham is busy and everyone is Indian. Rina *behn* grumbles as she tries to park in a space between two cars. Her car makes warning noises and Sonal shouts when she thinks the car will hit the other one.

'Oh damn! That was close,' Rina *behn* says.

They get out of the car and walk past Kumar Silks where Sonal once bought a *salwar kameez* for Diwali. They walk past Saravana Bhavan and see the queues lengthening. Two days after arriving in London, Kuresh had brought Sonal here to eat *dosas* and *sāmbhar vada*. The fruit shops are stacked with watermelons, mangos, oranges, just like home. In Tesco, fruit lies flat in boxes.

They leave their sandals outside the temple and walk up the wide steps. Inside, Sonal is claimed by the familiarity. Wide shiny marble floors and people, so many people. Some are walking round the deities, some sitting down before the shrine, some standing and talking. Women sell sarees in a corner. There are children playing; little girls dressed in shiny red *lehngas,* blue blouses, a mismatched spectrum of colours instead of the pretty pink of the frocks they wear at other times. They run around as if it's a playground.

She shows Rina *behn* where to queue and buy a ticket for the *puja.* They give you a plastic basket with a garland of red and yellow chrysanthemums, a stick of incense, a bunch of grapes, a red apple. Sonal had done a *puja* for five pounds when she'd realised she was pregnant, to thank the Gods and ask their blessings.

Sonal walks around the main shrine, touching the base of the deities enshrined in the wall. At the Shri Lakshmi alcove, she dips her forefinger into the vermillion red and marks the centre of her clavicle. A breastplate gleams on Lakshmi – shiny zirconia, blue, red and yellow, a colourful *saree* bunched at the waist. Her mother has suggested she do a puja, a ritual to calm Sarada, the village goddess whose anger has been irked and who destroys little ones in the womb.

Rina *behn*'s *puja* is over. She is ready to leave.

'Thanks Sonal…and you will be fine going back on your own, isn't it? I will see you next week, all right?'

'Yes, I will be fine. See you next week.'

Rina *behn* hasn't walked around the *Navagraha*, the nine planets. You have to circle them with brisk steps, either three times or seven. Leaving the temple without a prayer for the planets isn't good luck. She wonders if she should call her back, but Rina *behn* is probably already driving away fast, speaking to her husband and planning an evening out.

In Baroda, the Shiva temple was at the end of the road, the path to it often slushy so that her sandals were always caked with damp mud. She went there every Monday. It smelt thickly of stale flowers and incense. The *paduka* they offered was a light liquid, sticky on the palm, which you licked. Here, they don't offer it and they are careful that flowers don't stick on the temple floor. The temple is clean, almost antiseptic.

She walks to the tube. District line to Plaistow. From there she will take a bus to Sidcup. A young *gora* sits opposite her, smiling faintly while he looks his phone, fingers moving fast on the screen. A wide dimple on his cheek. When he leans forward, Sonal catches the smell of faint cigarette smoke. Perhaps she has made a sound, because he looks up and smiles briefly at her. His eyes seem kind, such a clear blue. Back home, the fairer you are, the more handsome or beautiful you are considered. Light eyes belong to the truly blessed. She finds herself looking at his hands and clean, well-groomed nails. Her own seem tired and she notices *haldi* stains under her nails. She imagines his hands on hers. She imagines him asking her how she is. She imagines him telling her that the formed-unformed being in her womb never knew that it wasn't wanted.

'Excuse me,' he calls after as when she gets up. He's gesturing towards her scarf lying on the seat, pink flowers studded on white. He holds it out to her and smiles. She mutters a thank you. Tears swell. On the platform, she looks back, wondering if he's looking at her, but his head is bent, back in his own world. Everyone in their own worlds. Everyone belonging.

She doesn't board the bus. Instead she walks, first to the right, then the left, left left, right, right, left, right, until she doesn't know where she is. The city is alien. She keeps walking.

Eventually she will reach home.

THE ENLIGHTENMENT OF RAHIM BAKSH

Nadia Kabir Barb

The water was almost scalding, just the way Mr Rahim Baksh of 92 Fernbank Road liked it. There was something purifying about the hot jets beating down on his body. He increased the heat until it was on the verge of being unbearable, then turned the thermostat the other way to its lowest setting. The icy water made him gasp. An invigorating mix of pain and pleasure.

After drying himself, he wrapped the towel around his waist and wiped the condensation from the mirror before shaving. He still favoured an old-fashioned shaving brush and cream. There was something very satisfying about the ritual of dragging a sharp razor across his chin, hearing the scrape of steel until he achieved the desired effect – a smooth, close shave. His old barber would have been proud of him.

For once, he regretted his limited collection of aftershaves and colognes. He rejected his favourite and most frequently used, Old Spice, leaving a choice between the Paco Rabanne and Aramis. After a couple of minutes of indecision, he opted for the former and sprayed it liberally. The intensity of the fragrance hit the back of his throat making him cough.

He stood staring at the row of shirts hanging in his wardrobe. They reminded him of soldiers standing to attention. Rahim Baksh believed clothes were for functionality not fashion. Had it been any other day, he would have reached for the clothes most easily accessible, the trousers that were at the top of the pile and the shirt on the end of the hanging rail. He repeatedly wore the same clothes, something that until today had not bothered him.

He took his time surveying the garments, his hand lingering over a white shirt before selecting a dark blue-and-white checked one. Then he pulled from the bottom of his pile of trousers, a pair of denim jeans. Even as a young man, he had never been partial to or comfortable in jeans, but his life was about to change, and he felt that this should also be reflected in his appearance. It was to be both an internal and an external makeover. Despite having put on a few pounds, he was relieved to be able to get them on. He had forgotten that the jeans had been a size too big for him in the first place.

There was a 'pinging' noise from his mobile. It was a text message from Karen. His heart beat faster. How strange that just her name should create this excitement. *Have the book I promised to lend you, see you later.* What caught his attention more than the words or the smiley face was the 'x' at the end.

A kiss. She had sent him a kiss. He closed his eyes and took a deep breath and imagined her heady perfume. He could almost feel her full lips pressed against his own. The kiss, albeit virtual, strengthened his resolve. He had waited long enough. It was time to declare his love for her.

A quick comb of his thick hair and he was ready. These days there were more flecks of grey than he would have liked. A trip to the pharmacy to buy hair dye had ended with him too embarrassed to hand it over at the counter and he had left empty-handed. His pride had outweighed his vanity.

At the book club, during one of the many animated conversations, Richard, a colleague from the IT department, had lamented the lack of bald protagonists. 'Hair-ists, the bloody lot of them, I tell you,' he had joked. 'Name a hairless hero if you can.'

Karen had jumped in. 'You know, bald men are thought to be very sexy. Look at Sean Connery and Bruce Willis and Ben Kingsley.'

'Patrick Stewart!' Janice had giggled.

'They're actors, not characters in a book. See you can't name one!'

'Who cares?' Karen flashed him a smile. 'They're still sexy.'

'Well, in that case, I feel better already,' Richard had laughed, rubbing his balding head.

Karen had turned to Rahim and whispered with a wink, 'Lucky is the man who has his hair beyond the age of forty.'

It had become somewhat of a mantra for him. On the north side of his fifties, he still had a full head of hair, unlike some of his contemporaries.

He shook himself back to the present. Walking downstairs, he was aware of the clattering of plates and the bubbling of a kettle. The kitchen was to the right but first he had to manoeuvre himself past the coat rack which heaved with outer garments. The stand appeared to have a life of its own, multiplying and growing. In most households, people complained of socks disappearing in the washing machine, a domestic Bermuda triangle. Once inside the machine, there was no knowing how many would come out. In his home, the coat rack was going in the opposite direction, multiplying not subtracting.

His wife Shaila was in her dressing gown. It used to be a vibrant primrose yellow but had faded to the colour of jaundice, an unbecoming shade that made her look sallow. The robe was the third member of their twenty-four years of marriage.

She was armed with a frying pan and spatula.

'Tea's nearly ready and I've made an omelette for you.' The said omelette was deposited unceremoniously onto a plate.

'Two toasts or one?'

'Two,' he replied.

He took a knife and fork from the cutlery drawer and ripped a sheet of kitchen towel from the roll, folding it neatly into a triangle. He sat at the small kitchen table and began to butter his toast.

'Have you eaten?' he asked.

She nodded and sat down on the other side. The smell of fried onions clung to her dressing gown. He wished she would throw the damned garment away.

'*Jaan*, don't forget we have lunch with Shahed and Margret tomorrow,' she said taking a sip of her tea. In the early days, he'd tried to suggest she use *darling* as a term of endearment instead of *jaan*. She had laughed and dismissed it. After a while he had given up.

'I thought I could make some *halwa* or *kheer* to take with us but can't decide which. What do you think?'

He wanted to tell her he couldn't care less what she made as he wouldn't be joining her the following day or any other day. He wished she was more like the wives of his friends or colleagues.

In all the years they had been married, she had never baked a cake or made some biscuits. It was always *halwa* or *kheer*.

He shrugged and said, 'You decide.'

He had lain awake most of the night trying out different ways of telling Shaila he was leaving her. 'I don't love you anymore' felt harsh but so did 'I'm in love with someone else.' After all she was the mother of his two children. He thought about the 'it's me not you' excuse but rejected it. What worried him more was breaking the news to his son, Shabbir, and daughter, Aneela, both at university. He had no idea how they would take it. He hoped Karen would be able to advise him on how best to deal with this rather delicate situation.

'I'm a bit worried about Malcolm. I haven't seen him for a while. Do you think he's OK?' Shaila asked, frowning.

'How am I supposed to know? I'm sure he's fine. These homeless people don't stick around in one place.'

'I wanted to give him some of the rice and *korma* I made. Even the people at the supermarket haven't seen him.'

Malcolm was a vagrant his wife had befriended and supplied with meals on a regular basis. He was worried that one day he would come back from work to find Malcolm ensconced in the house wearing his dressing gown and bedroom slippers. He was quietly relieved the man had gone elsewhere.

'What time is your book club today? You know I was thinking I should join too. We could go together,' she said, not waiting for an answer.

'Twelve.'

'What are you reading now?' He wished she would stop asking questions. It was more an inquisition than a conversation.

'It's a book by Kazuo Ishiguro. You probably won't have heard of him,' he replied, looking up from his toast and omelette. 'He won the Man Booker Prize in eighty-nine.'

'Oh, didn't they make a film of his book? What was it? *Remains of the Day* with Anthony Hopkins. I love him. So distinguished, don't you think *jaan*?'

Rahim frowned. 'Yes, but we're not reading *that* one.'

She nodded and mouthed an 'Oh.'

He had been at the book club for a year when Karen had joined eight months ago.

'You're wearing jeans!' Shaila sounded incredulous as she stared at his legs. 'Are you feeling alright?' She laughed and touched his forehead.

Her laughter rankled. 'It's better than wearing that thing,' he said, pointing at the dressing gown. 'Have you looked at yourself in the mirror recently?'

His jibe found its mark and her smile vanished. She looked hurt and he felt satisfied. Shaila's simplicity had been endearing at first and her love for all things Bangladeshi had amused him. Now he found her lack of sophistication and *deshi-ness* embarrassing. She seemed plain and unremarkable. A middle-aged woman with a penchant for Hindi serials and cooking.

All those years ago, when his mother had placed Shaila's photograph in front of him, he had been taken with her big eyes and wide lips. Not beautiful in a conventional way but a pretty little thing. He had agreed to meet her and was even more impressed in person.

Unlike the other girls paraded in front of him, most of whom were shy and tongue-tied even when asked the most banal of questions, she possessed a quiet confidence.

On their first meeting, she had been candid and expressed her desire to live abroad, something Rahim could offer her. Rahim wanted a wife who would adapt to life in England and provide a home for him and his children when the time came. It was to be a mutually beneficial union. With his newly acquired British citizenship and his job at a firm of accountants, he was quite the catch. Shaila's family and his own were equally enthusiastic about the match. His family was relieved he had agreed to marry a Bangladeshi girl, not one of the English students he was infatuated with during his university days.

He soon realised that an arranged marriage did not lend itself to romantic encounters. There were no stolen kisses nor passionate embraces prior to their wedding night. She was less adventurous than he had thought and they had always met under the sharp vigilance of one of Shaila's relatives. Their courtship had been brief and they had married within a couple of months.

He ate the rest of his breakfast in silence as he contemplated spending the rest of the day with the woman who had reignited his passion. He soon found out that his wife was an unexciting bedmate. Even in the early days, she switched off the lights before climbing between the sheets. He wondered whether during their infrequent love-making, she lay there formulating recipes or creating shopping lists. Her wifely duties were fulfilled with the enthusiasm of an automaton. It was no wonder his attention had wandered.

He recalled Rachel from the office. She was the temporary receptionist whose low-cut blouses were such a distraction that Rahim was unable to concentrate when she was around. Then there was Naomi, the nurse at his GP practice. Her trim little body in her white uniform made his body react in a way his wife no longer did. He hadn't had the nerve to say anything to either of them but he wasn't going to make that mistake again.

'Will you be back for lunch?' Her voice broke into his thoughts.

'No, don't wait for me. I'll get a bite to eat with the others from the book club,' he replied as he got up to deposit his plate in the sink. Mancini's would be a good place to take Karen for lunch unless, of course, she had other preferences. He felt like a teenager embarking on his first romance.

He put on his coat and made sure he had his phone, wallet and keys. The umbrella was rejected as too cumbersome. England and the unpredictability of its weather was one of the very few complaints he had regarding his adopted homeland.

The air was crisp and bracing. He took a deep breath and smiled. Not long till he was with Karen. He had taken to arming himself with a newspaper to alleviate the boredom of the forty-five-minute bus ride. The journey was one reason why he had decided to stop going to the book club.

'Hello there! Long-time no see. How have you been sir?' asked Mr Patel, the owner of their local newsagent.

'Very well, thanks. How's Mrs Patel?' He recalled her having some surgery. He couldn't remember if it was the knee or hip.

'The doctor said the recovery is a slow process but she's doing OK. Mind you, she's loving the attention!' Mr Patel said with a smile that revealed the ever-growing gap in his front teeth. Rahim was none the wiser as to the operation.

'I haven't seen the kids for a while either.'

'They're up in uni. Not back till next month.'

'How time flies,' Mr Patel shook his head. 'Say hello to the Missus and thanks for the samosas she made. The kids polished them off by the time I got home!'

'Will pass on the message,' Rahim lied, waving as he left the shop and walked to the bus stop. Shaila appeared to be feeding the entire neighbourhood.

He didn't have to wait long. The bus was almost empty and he had the luxury of choosing a seat. He went to the back and opened up his paper. After a few minutes of flipping through the pages, he admitted defeat and stared out of the window.

Their book group had been brought together by Simon, a colleague from work who had roped him in and for a while he found it interesting. When Karen joined, she had introduced herself and asked if she could sit next to him on the sofa. He nodded and from then on had ceased to concentrate as her knee kept brushing against his own. He told her he was thinking of leaving during the tea break.

'Not on my account, I hope,' she joked and touched his arm.

That was the last time he thought of leaving. Instead, he became one their most regular members. Karen injected new life and her exuberance brought colour to his drab existence. In her thirties, she was by far the youngest of the group.

He checked the time, realised he was early and decided to walk the slightly longer and more scenic route to Simon's house. It would give him the chance to figure out what he was going to say to Karen though that would have to wait until after their book club gathering had ended.

He had over the last few months accumulated and stored in his memory every touch, every smile, all their conversations. He wondered if he would be able to sit near her without giving in to the desire to pull her against him and kissing her. He laughed out loud. That would be scandalous.

He stopped at the zebra crossing and looked across the street.

111

The laughter died on his lips. He didn't have to see her face to know it was her. The familiar grey coat, the blonde hair tied in a ponytail, the big black bag she always carried. Only she was kissing Richard while his arms encircled her waist. They were too caught up in their passionate embrace to notice him. He felt winded.

He turned around and walked as fast as he could to the bus stop. He perched himself on the edge of the red plastic bench beside the other people waiting. He sat there watching the passengers get on and off, counting the buses go by…eight… nine…ten. It was only when his back started to ache that he boarded one. It was the twelfth. The journey back felt interminable, longer than usual with the houses and buildings going past him in slow motion. From his window, London appeared miserable.

He entered the house and shut the door behind him as quietly as he could. The television was on in the living room. Judging by the sound track, Shaila was watching one of her Hindi serials.

'Is that you, *jaan*?' she yelled.

He hadn't been quiet enough.

'Yes, feeling a bit tired so I'm just going to go and lie down,' he shouted back as he made his way upstairs.

He sat down on the bed, his body sagging with weariness. He touched the fraying fabric of the yellow dressing gown thrown over the pillow. It felt safe and familiar.

There was a 'ping' from his mobile. *Missed you at the book club, hope you're ok. Will give you the book next time.* This time the 'x' at the end of Karen's message appeared to mock him. How free and easy she was with her kisses and affection. He closed his eyes, only this time the image of her body pressed

112

against Richard's played like a video on loop. He walked into the bathroom, took his clothes off and turned the thermostat right up.

Rahim stood under the shower and waited for the water to hit his body.

First published in the short story collection Truth or Dare – Nadia Kabir Barb (Bengal Lights Books) 2017

NATURAL ACCENTS

Mona Dash

After twenty years of living in a country where the sun rose and set at wildly different times depending on the season, and the clocks were changed to ensure a semblance of light when people woke from deeply dark nights, Renuka decided she must acquire a pukka accent. An English accent. She had just turned forty. She had the detached house set at a respectful distance from the street, a large garden with roses and apples, a pond where fish swam to the splashes of a little boy-statue weeing, hedges bursting red and orange in the autumn, a career in a media company, ISA accounts warming nicely in the bank, the children in private schools, the successful, doting husband, Joe Malone candles on side tables, Chanel and J'adore bottles on her dresser, diamonds on a ring, and rubies on gold chokers gleaming in a safe under the floorboards.

But that accent.

When she spoke, she sounded from elsewhere, from somewhere beyond this green and pleasant country with its Brexited brass walls. She sounded as if she came from across the seas like the *Lord of the Oceans*, the ships that had departed Britain's shores, spent weeks at sea, and returned with cotton, indigo and spices. Later they came with people; their lives and dignity. The accent came from some part of the tropics, a large country where the sun rose and set at the same time no matter what the season, where time was sacred and clocks were never tampered with. Grown in one country – hot, fertile, and dusty – and transported to another – rainy, green and grey – this accent couldn't shake off its roots.

Once in Soho, she'd asked a passer-by for directions to a restaurant. The bemused man answered in his sing-song Welsh accent, 'I am an outsider like you. I am lost as well!'

'But I am a Londoner,' she told him, even as he continued smiling, not comprehending. She knew this city well. She had been drunk, she had ranted, she had celebrated, she had kissed in London's streets and parks. It claimed her, it shaped her. She didn't know where this specific street was, but it was nothing to do with being an outsider. She wanted to tell him this, but he walked away trying to find his own destination.

Or the time she mentioned to her colleague that she was planning a weekend away in Paris.

'Pardon me, where?'

'Paaris.'

'Where was that again?'

'You know Paaris? The tale of two cities? Eurostar? France?

'Oh, sorry, Pharis! I am sorry, I just didn't get it.'

'Yes, Pharis.' An imaginary h, a wide aa, so much more befitting the city of lights.

Back in India, relatives questioned, 'You have lived in England for twenty years but how is it you don't have an accent?'

'I do have an accent, an Indian accent.'

'Yeah, but surely you should have an English accent by now?'

'I am happy with the way I speak.'

'My friend went to America, and in two years he was speaking just like them! And you, you have been there so long…'

A couple of years ago, their new nanny, Megan, asked, 'You know, you speak quite good English, so when did you learn the language? Was it when you came to England?' Megan was making roast chicken for the kids' dinner. Her glasses steamed over as she opened the oven door and checked the half-cooked bird.

'Well, I always spoke English,' Renuka knew she sounded defensive. 'Most Indians speak English.'

'Oh, is that right? Why do people in India know English?' Megan asked, her face a mask of concentration as she plunged the knife deep into the heart of the bird and attempted to cut off the legs.

'The British were in India for years, don't you know? Ruling it, like for some two hundred years?' She heard the sarcasm creep into her voice.

'Oh yes, of course,' Megan said absently. 'Dinner is on the table! Anita, Arjun!'

Efficient, loving Megan who didn't know anything about the busy gallows hanging men to their death and the *Vande Mantarams* that blazed through India years ago or the reason the land was split and seared across.

That night, she told William and he laughed, 'Why did you not mention you studied English in Oxford?'

'Would that help? She thinks if you don't speak English the way the English do, you are a foreigner.'

'Look, we all sound different. How does it matter?' His broad

Australian accent, the childrens' clipped British, her polished Indian. William had been brought up in the outback of Australia, on an immense farm so impossibly far from any other part of the world. Like her, he too had come to England to study and stayed on, his language learning the English ways, but his accent drawling on with its idiosyncrasies. Unlike her, he didn't care. The coral reefs, the open air had shaped his calves, his arms, his jaw.

There had been a time when she had thought about having a tummy tuck and spent days skimming through magazines to find the perfect treatment. She held the loose skin on her stomach in a roll and imagined it flat and smooth like marble. Brown skin is more prone to stretch marks than white skin so she could never be like the mums of four that sported bikinis, but if her stomach didn't carry the scars it did, didn't carry the signs of having her two gems, would it not make her less real? She never went ahead with the tummy tuck. But the more she thought of it, and she thought about it often, the more she wanted to acquire a better accent.

Some of Renuka's friends put on accents, like a quick smear of lipstick. 'Hellow,' they said into their phones. In restaurants, they sharpened the ta in a word to a rubber-band snap. 'May I have the penne pas-*tta*? The *tt*a-lia-*tt*elle for me.' But the feigned accent quickly fell limp. Renuka didn't want a temporary accent that changed with emotion or tiredness or days or moods. She didn't want elocution classes where a tutor would train her tongue, commanding it unlearn what it had learnt as a toddler. It had to be ingrained, flowing in her blood. She had read about a new, fast way for foreigners to acquire a perfect accent. It was advertised in the Metro and various magazines. It was called The Natural Accent Shop.

She thought her thought, honed it and when perfected, told William. At first, he hadn't understood. They were having an al fresco dinner, the kids playing in the backyard, jumping in and out of the vast inflatable pool. It was one of those warm summer evenings one lived for in England, the ones that came rarely.

'It's the only way I can truly belong here. It's not the skin colour because there are enough British Indians around. Nor the clothes one wears nor the food. I can whip up strawberries and cream faster than anyone else, and make an excellent bread and butter pudding. I even like fish and chips and we have chicken tikka on a Friday evening which is as British as you can get. But people are obsessed with accents and as long as I speak English with my Indian accent, unless I sound exactly like the English, everyone will think I am a visitor. Always from somewhere else. Forever.'

'But I speak this way, and it doesn't worry me.'

'That's different.'

He continued looking at her with his half-smile.

'Well, you tick more boxes than me…white, male, Australian, a higher pecking order, you know.' She laughed.

'You are too harsh!' He laughed. 'If the accent is so important to you, why not? There's no harm in it.'

Exclusive and in the heart of London. Choose your own accent and walk out a different person, the website said. The photo showed a shop in Spitalfields, so much like Ollivander's wands in Diagon Alley where Harry Potter and his friends bought the perfect wand.

After work, the next day, she trailed along the market's confusing lanes. She found herself outside a *Nature's Soaps* and because the fragrance beckoned, she went in. The walls were lined with candles and baskets were filled with misshapen knobs of soap – rose, coconut, avocado, glycerine mixtures – all strewn on the exposed wood floor.

'Would you know...umm...where the accent shop is?'

"Pardon?' The man behind the counter asked. His hair fell long over his forehead.

'You know, the accent shop,' wondering if she was pronouncing it correctly. 'Accent, like how you pronounce things?'

'Hmm, yes.' His accent was a clouded Italian, very prominent. 'You mean Jim's shop? Just opposite. Look.'

He steered her around and pointed outside. Towards the left was a small shop with innocuous lettering saying *Natural Accents* in dark blue on a grey door.

The space was light-filled, thanks to the expanse of glass hewn into the old brick ceiling. On the wall was a large digital display of a map of the world in which countries came into view then faded as other countries took their place. Overlaid were words that sprang out of blue lakes and from mountain ranges, in different languages and different dialects. *Realize* and *realise* emerged from the USA and U.K. *Baby, bairn* and *baby* from Scotland, England and Wales.

'Hello, may I help you? I'm Jim.'

A tall, slight man, younger than she expected with wavy hair down to his shoulders. This was the way she wanted to speak, the words clipped neatly at the end. The perfect mix of sharpness and softness, just like the chocolate puddings she made with crisp exteriors and gooey insides. Liquid and solid.

'Hi, I am Renuka. I'd just like to know how it all works here... your services, I mean.'

'Welcome to Natural Accents. This is Harvey.' A little white robot emerged from a door on the right.

'Hi Renuka,' it said, its face crumpled as if it was smiling. She smiled back at it. No, at him.

'It's very simple. You choose an accent from our vast library, either out-of-box or customised. You decide semi-permanent or permanent. You know, like hair colour?' Jim looked at Renuka's hair for an instant, prompting her to run her fingers through her sleek curls, brown and blonde over the original black. 'Then we make a couple of small incisions in your skin. The depth depends on the accent type. Then we just insert one of these.'

He walked over to the counter and from a wooden box pulled out a minute circular object, like a watch battery but even smaller. 'We call this an accent box. You know like a voice box? We place them sort of here.' He ran his fingers down the sides of his neck.

'Goodness,' she said, before she could stop herself, her voice high.

He must have read her fear because he added hastily, 'It's not as bad as it sounds. The incisions are small. You won't even feel it, no more than a tattoo. Our facilities are in the heart of Harley Street.' He gestured towards more posters over the counter. 'The very best.'

The shelves behind him were labelled: Main Accents of the U.K: Received Pronunciation, Cockney, Scouse, Geordie, Scottish, Irish, Welsh. Below that were sub-accents.

'Is that BBC English?' She pointed at the Received Pronunciation.

'Ah this one, this will give you a traditional style of talking. I think they need to make a more popular one out-of-the-box, toss the RP in with a bit of today's London, but that's still on the roadmap.'

'How about something like yours?'

'Mine? Mine has a mild smattering of Irish.'

'Oh, I am sorry. I am not too attuned to different British accents,' she said hastily as Jim looked somewhat affronted.

'That's alright, but listen...*Brogue ...Hooligan...Shamrock...* can you hear the lilt in these words? I wanted to hold on to a part of my roots, hence the specialised accent. Would you want to toss in some customisation? It does make it a little more expensive of course. Well, almost double...'

Her budget was ten thousand pounds. She planned to pay it with her next performance bonus.

'I think out of the box is fine.'

'Fair enough, but first we need to know something about your background and your language preferences. Afterwards, we'll offer a free recommendation of the accent that best suits you. All you have to do is answer the questions Harvey asks.'

'In we go,' Harvey said, and she followed him into a room at the back.

'Like a changing room,' Jim winked, then went to greet the elderly man who had just walked in.

Once she'd agreed to the terms and conditions and declarations of privacy, Harvey asked her question after question:

Where were you born? Where are you from? What is the first language you spoke? What is your mother tongue? What is the primary language you converse in? Which language do you use in written communication? Which language do you think in? Dream in? Make love in? Are you married or in a relationship? Do you have children? What kind of an accent do they have?

When they were done, Harvey plugged himself to a printer and a report slid out. He left the room and handed it to Jim. Renuka followed him back into the main office.

'It does recommend RP but suggests some standard Indian and Cockney,' Jim said. 'It's like I said, you can consider adding layers to stay in sync with your roots. Have your tongue savour what it knows.'

'You sell Indian accents even?'

'Of course. That's the Indian section.'

'But who wants an Indian accent?'

'We get all kinds, and remember they can be temporary, so actors often come here. It's quicker than trying to master an accent for a role.'

'I don't want any more mixes. Just out-of-box please.'

'OK, this is the best quality. You won't even remember the way you spoke English before.'

'Right. That's what I need. A pukka accent.'

It was close to ten thousand pounds for an out-of-box top class perfect accent, with a thirty percent upfront payment. If you changed your mind within the first five days, you could revert to your original way of speaking. But once the accent box had settled firmly in, there was little you could do.

Jim had been right; the procedure was fairly simple. It would take a few hours for the accent box to settle into her throat before traverse the entire network of veins and helping her form words the way she wanted.

As instructed, she rested for a while, then read the dictionary aloud, perfectly. She pronounced names of countries and cities. When the family arrived home, she called out each of their names.

'William!' she said.

'You all OK? Are you allowed to speak already?' Even as she nodded, he said, 'Um…you sound…well…posh.'

'But that's good, right? What do you think Ani-tta? Aar-jan?'

'Why are you saying Ani-tta Mummy?'

'She said Arjan differently too,' Arjun protested.

'You sound like the teachers at school!' Anita said. Her voice was really small, like when she had left behind her teddy bear in Spain when on holiday.

'Arjoon,' she tried again, but it came out 'Aar-jan.'

'This is the way Mummy will sound now,' William said. She noticed the furrows on his forehead, a familiar sign that he was worried.

The next night, in bed, part way through a long kiss, William broke away and asked, 'Do you think they sort of changed the shape of your mouth?'

'No. Why do you say so?'

'Hmm, no, nothing, just felt a bit different.'

'I'm the same,' she reached towards him.

'Ah, mind your incisions. Maybe we shouldn't today.' He looked away.

'What's wrong?'

'Nothing, just a bit squeamish in case you bleed.'

'You've never been squeamish! And the cut has almost healed.'

'Almost, but you can't take the risk. Why don't we just go to sleep? Long day tomorrow. Goodnight, darling.' He turned off the lights.

Her husband had never said no nor switched off the lights.

She lay in bed, listening to him breathe. She mouthed all their names again. She sounded the same, didn't she?

On the third day, she went back to work. During a conference call, she didn't have to repeat a single word. People seemed to have developed a high level of comprehension. On the fourth day, her boss asked her to join an executive level meeting with their most important customer. 'We think you will be very useful with your knowledge and articulation.'

She texted William. Honey, the accent seems to be bringing other benefits!

On the fifth day, she called a friend in India to wish her a happy birthday.

'Hey, you sound so posh, so English! *Pura angrez ban gayi.*' Nysha squealed.

'Not at all, I am still the same person.'

Fresh giggles from Nysha, 'I feel I am listening to the BBC. Good *yaar*, when did you learn to speak like that?'

The sixth day was Saturday when her morning ritual was to call her parents in Odisha.

'Hello Ma.'

'Renu, is it you? Why are you speaking like this?' her mother asked.

'Do you have a cold?' her father said.

She could envision them seated on the blue-patterned sofa, phone on speaker, eager to listen to her voice, their only child. Their home hadn't changed in the last twenty years. When they travelled to visit her, it was always with trepidation and curiosity about the Australian son-in-law and the mixed children, one light-eyed and brown-skinned, the other dark-haired and light-skinned.

'I am fine, just...'

'But why are you speaking Odia like an Englishwoman?'

She heard her father chuckle at that. Why were her Odia words not sounding her own anymore?

'Ma, let me call back. OK?'

Renuka called Jim.

'How's it going, my lovely? You sound great.'

'Thanks Jim, I am fine, but this has changed a lot of things. I can't say Indian names. I don't sound the same when I speak Odia.'

'Pardon me? Odia?'

'My mother tongue. You didn't tell me it would affect other languages.'

There was silence for a minute. 'You didn't tell me you spoke another Indian language?'

'I am an Indian. Of course I speak another Indian language. In fact, I speak three.'

'Did you tell Harvey?'

'I don't think he asked...wait. I think he did ask about my mother tongue. Then what I spoke most in...I said English ...which is true, but wait....'

Jim interrupted, 'Hmm, maybe you didn't take the multilingual questionnaire. Yes, that must be it. You took the standard one which doesn't include all the sub-sections.'

'Jim! I took the one you set up.'

'Did you answer correctly then? Sorry, well, why don't you come over and we can see what we can do. It's only been five days.'

'It's the sixth day today.'

Jim whistled. 'Is it now? Well, come over as soon as you can.'

Renuka rushed out of the house. Anita was at a birthday party and William had taken Arjun to play football before picking up Anita. She didn't have to tell them yet.

What is your primary language? Harvey had asked. English. Wasn't that the language she thought in, the one she wrote in, the one she spoke and loved in, even when she had lived in India? English, the legacy she had acquired, the language she liked the most. But should that love take away something from her core?

Renuka reached Spitalfields, rushing, ignoring the smell of roast almonds, the soaps, a sensuous fragrance stall that seemed to have mushroomed overnight.

'Jim, what can you do?'

He smiled helplessly, 'Just add overtones of Indian English that might help with the names. And maybe the mother tongue. It may just...'

'May? Just may? Aren't you sure?'

'Look, this hasn't happened before. I did tell you it's the best quality and would completely change the way you speak.'

'But it was only supposed to change my English! That's all I wanted.'

'Let's calm down. Don't worry, we take full responsibility. But could you try and say a few words in this language, Odia you said? Have a go at – My name is Renuka and I live in London.'

The words took time to form.

'*Mora na* Renuka *aau mu* London *re ruhe.*' It sounded different. It sounded unreal.

She watched Jim pick several boxes from various drawers and stare at them. 'Yes, sounds like more than a hundred degrees of separation between the two languages, hence such a strong effect. You see, the closer languages sound, the less the effect. Harvey, can you come here and help please? We need to map out the degrees, mate…'

Harvey slid over and Jim continued, 'One of this, two of that, let's see, I could get an Odia accented English…and maybe dilute the RP. It should work. Stay calm, Renuka. Let's just hear you again?'

Renuka whispered, '*Mora na* Renuka *aau mu* London *re ruhe*,' over and over. Jim and Harvey joined in with her, the words, like a chant, filling the air.

First published in Leicester Writes Short Story Anthology 2018 (Dahlia Publishing, UK)

MRS BASU LEAVES TOWN

Reshma Ruia

Mrs Basu crouches in her seat at the airport gate
Chewing rat-like the ends of her sari
Bullet voices ricochet around
She grins confused like a fool
Cameras flash
A police woman scowls
Moves closer
Bare white legs pimpled with cold
Throw us a smile Mrs Basu thinks
Her bladder aches
Eyes sting from lack of sleep
She'd never wanted to leave her village far behind
It was her nephew's daft idea to make some money
Now her life-savings gone fed into
The hungry pocket of the middleman
Curled like a foetus living behind the kitchen door
Minding a stranger's child when she should be home
Sitting in the courtyard oiling her daughter's hair
Illegal alien to be deported Section 3(c)

The policewoman snarls
'I have a name' Mrs Basu shouts
'*I am Kamala Basu tenth class pass*'
Her mouth twists in anger
But she pats her heart and whispers '*Be glad*'
They hustle her to the back of the waiting plane
Where passengers fidget glower and swear
Strapped in her seat Mrs Basu lets out a sigh
She is finally going home

SMALL FISH

Deblina Chakrabarty

'How can you be scared of fish? Aren't you a Piscean?'

'What does that have to do with anything?' He didn't disguise his contempt for star signs as he reached for his cigarettes on the side table. The sheets would reek of smoke but he didn't care. He didn't live here long enough to notice odours or put up paintings.

'I don't know. I thought it might at least immunize you from fish phobia,' I laughed, reaching for a drag.

'It's not funny. I've hated them since I was a kid. Bloody grotesque creatures, bulging eyes, pulsing gills. Ugh.'

It was touching really, that he could be scared of something I wasn't scared of. This man who could catapult hacks and novices, even murderers, into political power with mathematical precision in the chaos that was Indian elections. It made me feel like I had an edge over him, however slim. It made us equal players in this game of cat and mouse. Well, cat, mouse and fish!

'So you don't eat fish either? What kind of a Bengali are you?'

'Huh, why wouldn't I eat them? I just don't *like* them.'

'Oh, I get it. No fish market visits for you then, no pressing and prodding to determine the freshness of the catch before the haggling? Let the proles do the dirty work and bring *sahib* a grilled fillet with some lemon butter on the side?' I couldn't help ribbing him. He wasn't the first person I knew who ate boneless chicken breasts or fish fillets crumbed, coated and deboned until all fishiness had disappeared. A country where elections were fought on vegetarianism was teeming with carnivores in denial.

I should have sounded more sympathetic since he was finally admitting a vulnerability to me, no matter how trivial. Every vulnerability was a currency of intimacy between us ever since I had allowed myself to become his sometimes-girlfriend (Delhi jurisdiction only) when he was in town. He responded with pressing and prodding of a different kind. As always I submitted. Not a protest in sight, even a feigned one.

It was almost noon when we sat down naked with our coffees in the sparse living room. The Delhi sun knocked for entry against the bamboo blinds. Bish was alternating between his laptop and the phone. Sundays were work days when you managed election campaigns for hot-button states. The old caste math of Dalit/Muslim/Yadav was not enough. The deep pockets and war chests of the incumbent national party didn't translate into victories. This time it was one of the far-flung north-east states; the Seven Sisters as they are euphemistically referred to. The people we Delhites dismissively wrote off as 'Chinkis' except when it was time to assert sovereignty at election time.

How had I ended up here?

One party too many, I guess. That's what happens when you've lived in a city too long to be a visitor but not long enough to have the trappings that make it home. Delhi is an insider's city. Look past the malls, the flyovers, the swanky T3 that doesn't even need the suffix of 'airport terminal' with its frequent flying loyalists, and at its heart Delhi is a fortress – you're either in or wanting in. A not-so-*Purana Qila*.[1] From Civil Lines to Golf Links, from Hauz Khas to Habitat Centre, it's an incestuous playground of People Like Us. Working for in-house communications in the Events Department of an influential media group meant accidental and unearned access to the fringes of this fortress. How an English Literature graduate ended up doing press releases for classical music soirées and young entrepreneur awards never failed to amuse me on the occasions it didn't depress me.

Funnily enough I didn't meet Bish at a party where I could've labelled him as a state *satrap*, or a pseudo-intellectual or a political animal. Sure, it was a Jorbagh mansion but otherwise there were was nothing worthwhile about this gathering. It was an ordinary Thursday night and we were a bunch of semi-employed and some flagrantly non-employed men and women trying to get high and failing. Too much tension, not enough laughs.

And then Bish walked in with Stoner Rohit.

'Neighbour. Sometimes.' Rohit mumbled by way of introduction.

Bish was clearly not my age or thereabouts. His body resembled a Gaugin figure, a smooth brown slab that looked like it had been built in an *akhada* – those olden style mud-wrestling pits – rather than a gym. Those muscles were definitely not just for show. He didn't speak much but his smile reached his eyes. And mine. His dark lashes outlined his eyes like a kohl rim. I had to go home with those eyes. They glittered like a snake later that

---

1 Purana Qila literally means Old Fort and is a famous Mughal monument in Delhi

night back at his flat, as he gored me with their gaze through the inky void of the moonless night.

I didn't think it would last.

A night to remember. Or forget. That's all.

Except that it became a string of such nights. And I began to join the dots despite myself. Stayovers, drunk dials, post-coital conversations about work, musings on god, a shared love for Indian Chinese food. All these random data points ached to become a line or a graph no matter how jagged, a pattern hidden underneath the chaos that would reveal a landslide victory for impossible romance against the incumbency of sluggish hook-ups.

'I passed out once, you know, with a fish. I've never gone near one since.' Whilst I had been daydreaming, he had shut his laptop and crossed the room. He sat on the floor at my feet, back against the settee, playing with my toes. The sensation wasn't unlike a bizarre fish pedicure I had once tried at a cheap beachside joint in Pattaya, with the poor little mites darting between my toes to make dinner out of dead skin, but I wasn't going to tell him that!

'I was 14, living in Bombay. It was school holidays. My parents' friends in our building were going on holiday with their children. They asked my mum to keep an eye on their aquarium. It was horrible, green and algae-covered, containing a few sickly orange goldfishes. The metal frame of the sides was rusted, the neon light inside flecked with black spots. For the life of me I couldn't understand how this was supposed to be a showpiece.'

'Let me guess. Middle-class humdrum made you gag?' I tried to be facetious because this relationship didn't have a user manual for intimacy. I didn't want to experiment and botch it up. He slumped a little, his head tilted back into the gap between my legs as he continued musing to himself.

'One afternoon my mother was sick and couldn't go up to check the tank and change the water. It had to be me. She didn't take my fear of fish seriously anyway. So there I was with a bucket and a mug trying to scoop the fishes out and put them in the bucket while I cleaned the aquarium. I didn't want fish leaping around in my hands. I managed to get them out and into the bucket ok while I cleaned but when I went to put them back, one jumped out and landed beside me. I think I threw up and passed out. When I came to, I was lying in my own vomit with a dead fish, and water all around me. I couldn't tell anybody what had happened so I had to find a replacement. And the pet market inside Crawford Market is its own special kind of hell.'

I didn't know whether to laugh or shudder at the thought of this physically imposing, thick muscled man lying in his own vomit, felled by a goldfish. I tried to hug him as best as I could from behind, my breasts squishing against his scalp, my nose nuzzling his nape.

'Why couldn't you just tell your mum a fish died? She'd square it off with her friend. It wasn't even your job to clean the tank.'

'I didn't want my mother to tell her friend. I didn't want *her* – I think her name was Poonam – to know I was scared of anything,' he almost sounded wistful.

I was baffled, 'Why not?'

'Because she was the first person I had slept with three months before. She was somewhat attractive, somewhat bored. I was stupid and very horny. That's how these scenarios usually play out, I guess. I thought I was calling the shots, making her come all howling and screaming in those somnolent afternoons, and then one day she dumped me. Just like that. The code words stopped working. I tried accosting her in the lift once or twice but she pretended nothing had happened. Told me to concentrate on my exams! I wasn't going to let her know I had fainted and vomited in her house. I was already a rejected man. Some pride had to be salvaged.'

I shouldn't have been surprised. The folklore of the horny married Indian woman isn't a figment of febrile imaginations. Stifled sexual longings have found all sorts of outlets, no matter how staid the paisley print on the coverlet of social dos and don'ts. And yet I found myself resenting this Mrs. Poonam So-And-So. Her careless boredom had cost Bish his innocence and his pride. The boy she had spurned would never return. I'd never know him.

The remainder of the day wrapped us in its quiet embrace. The strange revelation seemed to break some of the ice that surrounded our non-coital moments. We laughed more than I can recall. We held hands as we walked to Khan Market. I bought him flowers for the bare flat. He bought me kulfi. He was leaving for Aizawl on a campaign trip next morning. Network would be spotty but he'd be back in three weeks, late on the Saturday. He emailed the service company that maintained the flat to send their cleaning service early on the day of his arrival so that they could let me in and I could be there before his flight landed. It was the Delhi version of giving someone a key to their flat. It was enough to make me unreasonably happy.

I should have stopped reading the gossip papers. It's not even page 3 anymore, more like page 33, it's so crammed with has-beens, almost-beens and never-beens. But there was my daily alert from www.queenbee.com. *Tyre Heiress Turned Charity Pioneer Bags The Elusive Catch – A Big Fish Called Bish!* There were more awful puns on hooks, lines and sinkers but my attention was frozen on the woman's air-brushed photo. Smooth dusky skin, a manicured unibrow, a string of Polkhi diamonds casually strung across a black t-shirt, the kind of image advertisers refer to as 'aspirational' and editors celebrate on magazine covers. In India's blistering summers, these are women who have never been dampened by their own perspiration. There are no honking cars ruffling their Zen-like composure, no exhaust fumes clogging their pores, no cheap takeaway food thickening their waistlines.

And she was from Bombay. Outside my jurisdiction. It all made sense.

He hadn't said much about his work but over the months I had figured out the political jigsaw puzzle-making he did on the fringes of our frenzied nights and bleary mornings. Even without political alliances or ambitions, his calculations had disturbing foresight and clarity. He was AI before AI. Then he threw in some cutting-edge data analytics and basically took a wrecking ball to the old election math, breaking down entire constituencies to statistical units, binaries to be converted or retained. Everyone who politically mattered in the city had him on their radar. He was bound to end up with tyre-heiresses. Moneyed, pedigreed, influential.

Too bad Bish didn't care for star signs. They can be quite accurate sometimes. For instance, my weekly prediction for Geminis on queenbee.com this week told me to 'expect the unexpected.'

And here I was again. Eliminated in the preliminaries despite a great audition.

I began to wonder if Cupid was actually Simon Cowell. Over

the past three years he had dismissed my bathrooms hums and operatic arias alike with equal nonchalance. I was a fool to think he'd be moved by this rendition of Aida that had been building up wordlessly in my heart. Don't get me wrong, I am a perfectly adequate Ms. Right Now. My phone address book full of first-name-only Karans, Mihirs and Ajoys (not to be confused with the Joys) was testimony to my tendency for promising starts, but they all wandered off before I could save the last name. My address book was a labyrinthine nightmare, never mind my heart.

The usual pattern of uncoupling threatened to rear its head. Angry WhatsApp's, blue ticks followed by silence, awkward calls, broken plans, automatic iPhone replies and a slow dissolve into nothingness. I rolled through all the Rules I had broken.

I should've waited till the third date to sleep with him.

Only my place not his. Never the full night.

I should've had 'the chat' after the fifth date.

I should've kept anal for later.

How we beat ourselves up, we modern women, bastions of the privileged hen coop in which we graze. Liberal education, foreign travel, corporate ambitions, Hollywood soft porn, social smoking, adulterated hashish, Beyonce-esque twerking with our wide Indian butts. At the heart of every 'Fuck him' lies a whimpering plaintive 'What's wrong with me?'

Over the next three weeks my coolness surprised Bish. I wasn't calling him at odd hours and replying to his messages before he finished typing them. I left them for hours, mostly because I didn't know what to say without giving my screaming heart away. He interpreted this as nonchalance, a move in the game. He sounded impressed and piqued. It didn't occur to him that I'd read about Unibrow. Or maybe he thought he could spin the arrangement to me. He'd made an art *and* science of the spin after all. It made me realise how easily deductible I was to him, like his electoral data. An agglomeration of behavioural and socio-cultural minutiae to be decoded, slotted and influenced.

The late afternoon sun played peekaboo through the bamboo blinds when I arrived at his flat on the designated Saturday afternoon. The cleaning company staff were silently going about their business, justifying the mighty sums they charged to maintain and service these spacious apartments in the heart of South Delhi for high-profile iterants like Bish. The wood flooring set off the pale *kalamkari* rugs strewn across the living room, hallway and foot of the bed. The sparse furniture was old, solid teak. No matter how hard the company tried to justify its steep rates, there wasn't much to clean.

Bish lived like a hermit. I laughed silently as I contrasted my crammed wardrobe to his evacuated one. I wondered what kind of wardrobe Unibrow had? A walk-in closet probably, filled with soft black t-shirts that cost hundreds of dollars, artfully slashed black jeans from new-age designer labels and discreet leather loafers whose sole had never seen Delhi dirt.

I waited for the cleaning company to leave before I went down to my car. The backseat of my tiny hatchback was a mountain of cartons and packets. Reversing into the parking slot had been a superhuman feat. Even with a rope round the box, the combination of carrying and dragging it up a flight of stairs was more exhausting than I had bargained for. I vowed to work out more as I panted my way up, and not just for the loose bits around my tummy. I needed another trip to get the smaller box and the packet but finally it was all in. I was home alone.

As the light faded to a golden peach, the houses around me stirred out of siesta towards evening tea and hurried preparations for dinner guests. Porch lights came on, garden chairs came out or went in, murmurs of chitchat and instructions laced the air.

I thought to get the technical bit out of the way first. I'm terrible at reading manuals, worse at following them. I would've killed for a cup of tea but Bish's kitchen was no help. No milk, no sugar, a sullen pile of teabags and not even an electric kettle. Thankfully I had a few hours to hand.

There was a fair bit of trial and error but I managed to put it all together. I had bought the smallest model. Apart from it being the cheapest, and lightest to carry, it was a model that accommodated just one occupant. I had resisted the urge to get the prettiest one – half neon pink; half mustard yellow. For this purpose, it would have to be a fat little goldfish. For old times' sake. I had chosen the model with green plants, black pebbles, some red flora. The lighting was concealed under the top lid as was the waterline, giving the promised halo effect. The entire thing lay placid and seamless, an undulating orb of light and liquid, gracefully swaying on the teakwood writing table. The orb cast its moonlike glow throughout the bedroom, colouring the sheets even whiter and softer. I remembered us mangled in the sheets three weeks ago. Feels like a lifetime.

Next, not wanting to crease the sheets, I sat on the rug at the foot of the bed to assemble the *tottwo*[2] sourced from the Bengali

---

2　Tray of gifts voluntarily exchanged between the families of the bride and groom prior to the wedding. These usually contain sweets and symbolic gifts for the bride and groom and their immediate families. *Tottwos* also often including a whole river fish, usually a *rui*, or carp – staple of the Bengali diet – as a centerpiece, dressed up as a bride. *Tottwo* bears no relation in spirit or execution to any demand or exchange of dowry wedding cottage industry operating inside CR Park. I realised I looked like an enthusiastic friend of the bride adding her special creative flair to ensure that the end result would outshine the assembly from the groom's side.

I had eschewed modernity for something traditional. Something befitting Bish. A typical red and white checked linen towel lined the wicker horse-shoe shaped rice sieve. Oranges, sweet limes and apples were scattered over with grains of rice. A silver tumbler and spoon were laid diagonally on one side, and the pièce de resistance lay in the middle, a rare 5 kg catch dressed as a typical Bengali bride, complete with a miniature red saree, a dot of *sindoor*, lashless eyes dotted at the rims with sandalwood and a *paan* neatly tucked into its gaping mouth.

I stood in the doorway and gazed at the room for the last time. It had been the seat of another hope for a happy ending. A womb of secret confidences, synchronized moans, awkward giggles, gentle snores. Now it lay bare, quiet and waiting. A goldfish was taking lazy laps around the silken plankton. The *tottwo* in the centre of the bed was lit by the ghostly light of the Biorb. The carp bride lay supine in its scaly splendour. A printout of the Queen Bee webpage sat like an instruction manual on the empty bedside table.

Maybe it was my imagination but I was sure I could read the words Big Fish in the headline even from this distance.

LETTER FROM THE GLASSHOUSE OPERA

Kavita A. Jindal

One way of looking at it
is to describe the splendour of this scene:
huge bay windows with leaded panels, steel vases
stuffed with blood-red roses on every ledge, and
the tall soprano's tunic in pea-green lace a-flutter.

An evening chill settles. Stoles are unfolded although
outside summer skies are light and burnished oaks
dot undulating emerald fields. Inside, Vittoria sings Schubert,
accompanied by a piano, two violins and a cello.
Tea lights flicker on the sills; the sickly smell of kerosene
wafts in as a gardener lights the braziers.

I understand no words of Schubert but
Vittoria is singing Sehnsucht.
I see it in her inconsolable hands.
These are the thoughts her refrain brings:

You are fodder.
Everything you say and don't say
will make it to the page even when it kills me.
You are fodder
and this is the straw I hold.
It is one way of looking at it.

I depict what my fervent eyes see
in this glamorous greenhouse
to keep a record of what I might have told you.
My head turns from violinist to cellist to violinist
so that the picture of you in a guerrilla fight
or in a wretched rebel cluster
or a hammer being taken to your head, to be exact,
that picture is not too sharp, not too obvious.
It is enough that I know what is happening there
and you will not be describing it to me.

The soprano sings on, pressing hand on hand.
She has the oddest big-jointed thumbs
but how she uses her heart to sing Mozart's aria,
the one he wrote for Nancy Storace;
when the singer had to depart Vienna.
He was dejected, or so the story goes.
Nancy was fodder; Mozart wrote an aria.
That's one way of looking at it.

JUNGLE DRUMS LEAD US

Kavita A. Jindal

On one side the study of biology
on the other white supremacy
Rivers run parallel, without dampening
the gravel spread between
Our wood is too desiccated to build bridges
because what narrative could reach across?

Genetics? Or the ancient paleness
of some nobility, and thus the loveliness
of paleness, or the other deeper fear
of a world overrun by people different to one;
with different eyes, cheeks, jaws, lips, hair.
Different language, wrong belief.

They are as pagan, are they not?
as all their ancestors were before
Christ saved them. In his name they
wield their banners forgetting he was a Jew
before he became anything else.
Born further east than they may acknowledge

Jesus possibly had dark hair and eyes,
his wanderings under the sun tanning
him further, had he been so fair
to begin with. This story can be hollered
across the chasm
if anyone's listening.

Paper planes bearing genome sequences
can be flown over the barricade
if anyone's reading.
The science: modern humans (that's us)
all of us, are descended from a single
founding population that left Africa

50,000 years ago. We are all African
in our cells. Even the fearful, the non-believers,
the "Purifiers", those who belong and
insist others don't. Might they be open
to learning something new
under the sun?

THE INVITE

Reshma Ruia

We receive an envelope with foreign stamps in the post. A piece of cream coloured paper bordered with red roses and violet hearts falls out. The invitation requests the humble pleasure of our company to celebrate the fortieth anniversary of....I stop. The card is from Anita. It is an invitation to her Ruby wedding anniversary party.

I feel lightheaded.

'What is it?' I hear Barbara's shrill voice. She's buttering her toast, eyes trained like binoculars on my face.

'It's from Anita. Remember my old college friend?'

Anita. Saying the name aloud feels strange, like the taste of a fruit whose name I forget.

Barbara pushes back her chair, comes around and leans over my shoulder, reading the invitation, mouthing the words in that annoying way she has as though she has just mastered the alphabet.

'Do we want to go all that way? The heat will be terrible,' she says, her forehead creasing.

'India is a hell of a long way to travel for a party,' I agree. There is a heaviness pressing against my eyelids and I shut my eyes briefly, picturing the party. There she is, Anita, wearing a magenta silk sari, her favourite colour, standing inside a big marquee festooned with marigolds and long trestle tables with buckets of ice-chilled wine and platters of food that smell of summer. Men run back and forth eager to be of service with keys to hotel rooms and air-conditioned cars that whisper wealth.

Anita has done it all herself. *A self-made woman, India's homegrown tycoon.* That's what her Wikipedia entry says.

'It's up to you, Peter, after all you're not needed in your office. I mean, you've stayed doing the same job for the past fifteen years.' Barbara arches an eyebrow and I feel her contempt travel down my spine. 'You've plenty of time on your hands, but the tickets won't be cheap and imagine if you fall ill. And what about the health insurance?'

Barbara pauses to brush fluff from her cardigan. The morning light catches her wedding ring, making it glint. She comes over and pats my arm. Her voice softens. 'Not sure why we're invited…I mean the woman hasn't spoken to you in years. Rent a crowd, I reckon.'

'I'm sure she's not short of friends. She's running a business empire. Good of her to remember us,' I murmur.

Barbara looks at my plate, at the half-finished omelette and the five crescent shaped apple slices in my bowl. 'Why have you stopped eating?' Her bottom lip quivers.

'Not really hungry,' I reply.

'I'll tidy up now.' She walks to the sink and wipes her hands on the kitchen towel.

'I'll do the clearing up, Barbara. You go and catch up on your gardening. Make the most of the good weather,' I say, not attempting to move. I know it will annoy her but this small act of defiance pleases me.

She stares out of the kitchen window, her hands still holding the towel. 'You're right. The flowers are spilling everywhere. I wish they'd bloom inside their borders.' She sighs and disappears into the utility room.

It's summer in London and the garden lies spread-eagled under a haze of honey sunshine. Through the open patio doors, I can hear the neighbour's children shrieking as they fill the paddling pool with the hosepipe. The shrubs and trees are alive with birds and the magnolia tree at the bottom of the garden wears its wedding dress of cream and pink flowers. I see all this and feel nothing. The invitation to Anita's Ruby Anniversary is like a dull shadow.

Barbara is back in the kitchen, gardening gloves on, gripping a pair of secateurs, ready to guillotine the dahlia heads.

'Is everything alright, Peter? You look pale.' She comes near me, one green latex gloved hand brushing my cheek.

All these years, and the touch of her hand still leaves me cold. I move away.

'Just my hay fever playing up. I'll take some Beconase.' I clear my throat and smile in reassurance.

'You'd better get cracking before the midges start.'

'Don't forget to tidy the kitchen. Rinse your plate and the fruit can go in the Tupperware, top shelf of the fridge, next to the cottage cheese. Not on the second shelf.' Barbara spells out her instructions a second time. She stops, narrows her eyes and examines my face. 'Are you listening?'

Orderliness. It's what she wants. The plates and the cutlery in the drawers are stored with military precision. Upstairs in the bathroom, the toilet rolls cower inside knitted crochet covers. Our clothes hang in colour-coded compliance in the wardrobe. At night, she sleeps with her body curled away from me in a perfect c-shape. Day after day, Barbara scrubs away at any sign of living that may interrupt our lives. Good job, we are childless. She would have found motherhood far too untidy.

I stand in the middle of the kitchen, confused about what to do next. I lift the card and hold it against the light, squinting to see if there's a secret coded message. *I have not forgotten you Peter.* I am vaguely aware of my wife, her portly frame bending down over the flowerbeds. A streak of white flashes across the blue sky as an airplane soars past. I check the card again and I am not here anymore. I'm back in the noisy cafeteria, sitting at the white Formica table, red faced and awkward, hunched over my mug of builders' tea.

'Do you mind if I join you,' someone asked. It was the first day of the first term of university and I was on my own in the cafeteria, too shy to join the gaggle of fresh faced first years chatting and laughing together.

I raised my head and there she was – shiny black hair, bright, long-lashed enquiring eyes and slim wrists jangling with silver bangles. I jumped to my feet, pulled out a chair, and felt a blush rise at back of my neck and travel to my face. I was a small town boy who'd come from a single sex school and felt uncomfortable around girls. Yet here was this striking girl in an orange dress asking if she could sit with me.

'Your food looks beige.' She pointed to my jacket potato with its film of grated yellow cheese. On her plate was a forest of lettuce, cucumbers and tomatoes.

'Yours is colourful.' I smiled and extended my hand, my thick pink fingers encircling her long brown ones. 'Hi, my name is Peter Barker and you must be …'

'I am still me.' She giggled. 'No, seriously, I am Anita Kapoor. I suppose you'll want to know more.' I nodded, still speechless. She continued. 'I am the eldest daughter of a zoo supervisor from Jaipur.'

With an introduction like that, I had to know more. She was studying abroad on a scholarship while I was the youngest child of schoolteachers from Cardiff. Our backgrounds couldn't have been more different.

'To be honest.' Anita leaned closer, her breath warm on my face, her hooded eyes deep with meaning. 'I hate the zoo. All those animals trapped behind bars. All they do is breed, eat, procreate and repeat. So unlike being in the wild. They need to be free.'

'I love dogs and hamsters,' I stammered in reply. How lame compared with her daredevil confession.

'They hardly count as animals,' she replied. 'I'm talking big here, elephants, lions, pythons. Ever seen a pair of pythons copulating?'

I shook my head. All I knew of life until then was playing hockey on a frostbitten grey pitch and accompanying my mother on her Saturday trips to Woolworths. And the occasional furtive cigarette with Jimmy, my best friend at school.

I began looking out for Anita in lectures. She rushed in, always late, folders falling, her hair a black cloudy mess. She could count on me to hand her the notes and lend her books from the library.

'Don't you have an alarm clock?' I teased her.

'Oh, but I have been up since five.'

'Doing what?'

'Completing my jigsaw puzzle of the Great Wall of China, that's what I've been doing. It has nearly a thousand pieces and is devilishly hard. I know you'll bring me up to date on trade tariffs during the Cold War.' She grinned and squeezed my arm. 'My dependent, solid, pink cheeked knight.'

That was Anita. Always full of surprises. I could not put her in a box or stick a label on her. *Her pink cheeked knight.* The description makes me smile even now, after all these years.

In the second year, we decided to rent two rooms together in Bloomsbury in an old Georgian block off Mecklenburg Square. The rent was low and we could walk to campus, saving on the bus fare. Bloomsbury was rough those days. Tramps with bandaged feet hid in doorways, cursing god. Our rooms were threadbare with sash windows that bled drafts and radiators that spat out bursts of warmth.

'Victorian poverty that Dickens would be proud of.' Anita's eyes were smiling slits of amusement. 'You Brits are good at ruling the world but can't manage a simple sink with a mixer tap.'

My parents visited from time to time. They hoped I would get a First and join one of the American multinationals that were setting up in the city. I had other plans. I wanted to be a writer.

'A moon-gazer in the garret,' Anita mocked, screwing up her face. 'I'll speak to your parents and persuade them to let you change your degree to English literature so you can starve in style.'

They did meet but not in the way, I imagined.

I swim across those lost years until I am back at the George and Dragon with my parents. The air stinks of beer and vinegar. I have invited Anita to join us because it's her birthday and she's a million miles from home. My mother has baked a chocolate sponge that takes pride of place on the laminated table. I watch Anita charm my parents through the evening. 'Such a perfect cake. Have you always been fond of baking?' she asks my mother. Anita is wearing her going-out batik dress and the blue eyeshadow on her eyelids makes her eyes browner. The talk moves to cricket and democracy in India.

'It's the country of the future,' Anita assures my parents, her eyes flashing pride. She winks at me and changes topic. 'Wouldn't it be great if Peter became a writer? The next Graham Greene perhaps.'

Father shakes his head and pats Anita's arm kindly, telling her that writing won't pay the bills. Mother smiles, her right hand holding the spoon dips in and out of the soup bowl. She dabs at her mouth with an embroidered handkerchief.

A group of young men enters the pub, their voices rowdy and their faces flushed with drink. We ignore them.

When it's time to cut the cake, my mother says, 'But we need candles!' Her hands fly to her face in bewilderment.

'How foolish of me to forget. Peter, be a dear and ask the bartender if he has any.'

I do as I am told but the drunk men are hogging the counter. They won't let me through. I jab the one nearest to me and he snarls and turns around, teeth bared, eyes pink-flecked in rage. 'What the fuck do you…' He pushes me and I stumble, falling backwards, my head about to hit the floor when arms grab me, breaking my fall. Anita has come to my rescue. She glares at the men, my head cradled against her shoulder.

'How dare you?' She shouts.

'Well, well, well…who have we here?' The men snigger and form a circle around us, closing in until their sour, beer-laden breath fans our face. Someone sets up a chorus of monkey noises.

'Who have we here…Black Beauty?'

'Go back to your jungle.'

'We don't want your kind here.'

It is over as quickly as it started. My father and other men rush in and manage to get the men thrown out.

'A performing monkey! Good job they didn't know my father owns a zoo,' Anita says, later that evening. She sits on the edge of my bed, her foot restlessly tapping the floor. The burning tip of her cigarette is the only point of light in the room.

'They're losers. Forget them. They don't count,' I say. 'I am sorry you had to see such ugliness.'

She shrugs. 'It's your mother I feel sorry for. Such a fine lady having to see that scum. And the bloody cake, we didn't even get to eat it.'

'Thank you for coming to my aid.'

'I'm your knightess in shining armour,' she says.

We begin to giggle.

My hand slowly creeps up and traces the outline of her face. My fingers linger over the smooth plane of her cheeks, the little cleft in her chin, the soft, unshed tear that hangs at the corner of her eyes. Anita takes my hand and presses it against her lips. I throw back the sheets and shift closer against the wall to make room for her.

First love. It remains a lifelong, unfinished business. The ache of it. The sweetness of it never completely vanishing. It was easy to hide away in a small room, skipping lectures, venturing out only to buy milk or the papers or a loaf of bread. We were dead to the world and alive only to each other.

I came back from the campus one day to find Anita in tears. Her father had suffered a stroke. The family needed her back.

The evening before her departure, we huddled close in front of the heater. 'You will come back, Anita. Promise me. I will wait for you.'

She nodded but her eyes were far away. 'We will see,' she said. 'But please don't wait. We should be free. Let's not put ourselves inside a cage. If it's meant to be, it will be.'

'But we love each other,' I whispered.

She sighed and turned to me, cupping my face in her hands. 'My dear, fragile Peter. You really should become a writer.'

She left London without finishing her degree. I waited for her to come back, failed my exams, repeated the year and graduated with a 2:2. In a few letters, she wrote about her new responsibilities. She had two younger sisters and she was the sole breadwinner. England was the past. 'Just look ahead, Peter. Don't ever let go of your dreams. Become a writer,' she told me.

Anita moved to Bangalore to work at a software company building microchips for American computers. It was all so different and strange and I couldn't relate to this new person – practical and ambitious. Somewhere along the way, she met a boy who worked in the same company.

A year later, Jimmy, my old school friend introduced me to Barbara who was tall and blonde and laughed at my jokes. She had a frightened, uncertain air about her that appealed to me. We rushed into marriage after she became pregnant. Three months later, she tripped on the front step and miscarried. She needed me more than ever. I became Barbara's pink-cheeked knight in shining armour.

'You've done the sensible thing,' Anita wrote. 'No point hanging on to the past.'

Over the years, her letters became infrequent but her memory lingered like a toothache.

'The dahlias are beheaded,' Barbara says, a pale smattering of pollen on her face and hair, as though she has taken a tumble through sunshine. Her small rabbit eyes dart around the room, take in the unwashed cups, the omelette congealed to rubbery yellow on its plate.

'Why is the kitchen still dirty? You're still holding the invitation!' She lets out a small cry.

'I was thinking of a suitable reply. I will send our regrets to Anita and tell her it's too far to fly and will be tiring for us.'

Barbara nods. 'That's what I said. It was enough that we attended her wedding.'

Anita's wedding day. We stand lost and confused, nodding and smiling as strangers offer us food and drink. It's difficult to reach Anita, surrounded as she is by family members, all talking and laughing. Barbara sticks to my side the whole time. She had insisted on wearing a sari to blend in and looks awkward and big in the blue silk that the hotel receptionist had wrapped around her. Her cleavage shines with sweat.

I elbow my way to the front, jostling and pushing, until I stand in front of the bride as she makes her way to the dais where the priest is waiting. I have a present for her. A thousand piece jigsaw of the Amazon rain forest. I want Anita to see me.

I want her to remember the old days. The sun and the alcohol have gone to my head.

She looks like a princess, all that silk, the jewels, her henna coloured hands holding up her long skirt. I lunge forward and grab her wrist. Startled, she shakes herself free, an eyebrow raised questioningly.

'What do you want, Peter?'

The women walking behind her are impatient. Someone nudges her forward and the moment is lost.

At the hotel that night, Barbara splashes water on my face and says I am an embarrassment. She stands in front of me, naked, the sari a puddle of blue at her feet. I can only stare at her, my limbs as heavy as stone. She turns the air conditioning full blast and collapses on the bed, her head drooping against the paisley-patterned headboard. Tears run down her face.

'Why can't you love me?' she says.

There's a clattering of pots and pans and the sound of running water. Barbara is making a performance of clearing the table. She drags the hoover from the pantry and sets it roaring, its cable snaking between my legs.

'Hey, are you trying to knock me over?' I fling my hands up in surrender. The noise of the hoover drowns out my voice. Barbara can't hear me. Her eyes are fixed on the damp patch on the rug – an old wine stain that will not budge. She comes nearer and snatches the invite from my hand, walks over to the cutlery drawer, takes out the scissors and cuts it into perfect little squares that fall like confetti into the bin.

'No point in hanging on to this,' she says, her lips sealed in a thin line.

WHERE HE LIVES

Kavita A. Jindal

I see him off at the front door. 'I'll try and meet you for lunch,' he whispers. 'Let me get into work, check what I have to deal with and I'll call to fix a time.'

I giggle. We feel like conspirators. Eight months married.

'But, Sabina,' Riyaz's tone is serious, 'go in now and eat a good breakfast. Don't play this game with me.'

So he'd noticed. This morning I'd let his mother set down his bhurji and parantha and watched like a good wife as he ate it. I was always hungrier than him in the morning, well, all the time, but my mother-in-law's repeated instructions had got to me. She hovered at mealtimes, over the cooker and over her son. She waved away her own comfort. Even when I'd tried, when I'd said, 'You sit down, Ammi-ji, and let me make breakfast for both of you,' she'd shaken her head. It was her kitchen and she knew what her son liked to eat. And pfft, I was so slow. A domestically untrained girl. She reminded me of my ineptitude daily. 'What use is philosophy, Sabina, when one has religion and tradition?' she asked. 'Philosophy is for people with leisure, with nothing to do in their lives.'

When I told my philosophy professor at the women's college, Mrs Palli, that I was engaged to Riyaz, she expressed displeasure. At the time I thought her discourteous. Wounding.

'Getting married,' she'd repeated with a sneer. 'You don't want to wait for a few years? Weren't you considering a PhD?'

'It doesn't interest me, ma'am.'

'But going to live in the old city with your boyfriend, that interests you, huh? You'll have to live by the rules of the old city, you know that?

'He'll be my husband then, ma'am.'

'You may love him but perhaps you're sacrificing your future for him.'

'He *is* my future.' She had no right to interfere.

Mrs Palli flapped her knotty fingers. 'You can wait a few years. You're young.'

'I'm already twenty-three.'

'You'll have to wear a burqa and niqab every time you step out. If Riyaz loves you, why doesn't he move to the new city?'

'His mother has been in that house for thirty-five years. She won't leave. I don't mind, ma'am, and that's what I told him. We'll be together every day, not meeting in secret, not hiding from the world.' It was all I wanted but I couldn't tell her that.

Her finger tapped the back of my hand. 'You don't understand what you're doing. They live differently in the old city. Women don't have any of the freedoms that you're used to. Do you realise how you'll be expected to dress and behave?'

'I am aware, ma'am.'

'I'm disappointed in you, Sabina.'

I hadn't expected that. The hurt must've shown in my eyes. I bowed my head, tears pricking. 'I'm disappointed in myself too,' I mumbled.

Why had I said that? Her apprehension and her lack of congratulations at my engagement had made me blurt that out. For a moment she'd made me feel desolate and uncertain about the clear-sighted decision I'd made.

I straightened my shoulders. I didn't need her approval even if I admired her. I loved Riyaz. Mrs Palli wouldn't understand. She wasn't young.

Her hands fluttered on my shoulder, as if she was brushing loose threads off a man's jacket. 'Forget what I said.' Her voice turned loud and angry. 'Forget it!' Then in a gentler tone, 'Good luck Sabina. Yes, yes, good luck.'

'Thank you ma'am.'

'Just one piece of advice if I may presume?' She didn't wait for permission. 'Riyaz is a fine young man. Enjoy your first few years together. Don't rush into having a child…'

My mother-in-law is a joyless creature. It's an unkind thing to say but is the truth always kind? *People need the truth about their world in order to thrive.* I used that sentence in an essay once. I got top marks. I used to be proud of that.

My mother-in-law likes me to stay home most of the day and do what she does. I help her in her chores. When she sits down with her coffee and listens to the local radio talk show or watches BBC World News on TV, I do the same. I know this is what is expected of me and I do it willingly, but I also need to get out of the house for a walk and to talk to my friends on my mobile. I need to be where she can't hear me. My mother-in-law doesn't like to see people having fun. It's vulgar. Next door to us lives a widow with a raucous laugh. Whenever I hear it, I long to find out what the joke is. My mother-in-law can't stand the woman's laughter. 'A widow,' she remarks, looking pained. 'Laughing so loud we can hear it on our terrace. No shame at all.' My mother-in-law is a widow too, a long-term widow. She wants next door to mooch about all day with downturned lips. 'Life isn't all fun,' she said to me one day. I think I know that. We all know that. That's why fun is important.

My mother-in-law likes me to sit with her at breakfast and lunch. Over breakfast she deliberates on what we will cook for lunch, just us two, and at lunch I get a monologue on what we will cook for dinner. What does darling son Riyaz long for? It wouldn't go down well to tell her that Riyaz longs for me and hardly cares what he eats. I'm the one more interested in food. Food is nutrition for body, mind, soul. As Virginia Woolf said, "One cannot think well, love well, sleep well, if one has not dined well."

Riyaz laughed when I quoted this to him. 'Love well,' he echoed. 'Make sure, *begum*, that I have the right food to love well.'

Sometimes I do escape in the early afternoon. Riyaz comes to the bazaar in his lunch break and I meet him there. Some days I'm happy and satisfied as we share snacks from the pushcarts. Other days I'm full of resentment and I punish him by going hungry. I see how his cheeks tighten and his lips close in held-in sorrow when I say I don't want to eat. I'm fed up. He understands.

Today when I see him, I'll declare: 'Let's go away for a holiday! For our anniversary. Goa!'

A beach. Just us. Floaty clothes. Prawn curry. Imagine. It won't happen, I know. Not yet. Riyaz has to save and Riyaz won't abandon his mother to waltz off with his wife. I'm working on her so that one day she will suggest it herself: 'Son, why don't you go on vacation to Goa?'

The phone rings. My mother-in-law hands it to me with faint disapproval. It's Mrs Palli. Her second call this week. She asks politely after Riyaz.

'He's doing great.'

Last time she asked me if I felt settled.

'Yes,' I'd replied. I knew I sounded sullen.

'Good, good.' Her confident cheeriness. 'If you're settled but not fully occupied, you should come back to study for your PhD. We're assessing applications soon.' A pause. 'You know my hopes for you, Sabina. You were my best student.'

I listen to her intensity today. 'The application deadline is next week. Have you considered it further?'

She wants to mould me into the next Mrs Palli. It was not what I wanted when Riyaz was top of my list, when I was sure I could adapt to anything, anything at all.

I look up at my mother-in-law who has stayed in the room and turned down the volume on the radio. She wants to mould me too. Who am I? What did I agree to be? Riyaz loved me for my exuberance and liberal mind, but now even he suggests that I could behave in a more reserved manner when I'm outside the home as better becomes a woman in a black mantle.

My mobile phone pings. It's Riyaz. 'Meet now at Bangle Bazaar crossroads. Sorry, got a bit late. Not much time before I have to get back.'

I half-run to the crossroads. When Riyaz finds me, I take hold of his chin in playful anger. I'm tugging hard at his short beard when a tourist with a big Nikon camera takes a picture of us. It's not the first time. I'm a slim woman in a silky black burqa and niqab, only my eyes visible, and I'm being un-demure. I look at Riyaz. He shrugs. We turn our backs on the tourist and his camera. Riyaz doesn't want confrontation. He never does. Even though the vendors in the market find the constant clicking tiresome, they never step in to admonish tourists either. They need all the business they can get. The outskirts of the new city, where the technology parks are, have become the draw with newly-opened malls and boutiques. Why come to the lanes of the old city unless you live here, have business or family connections here, or are a tourist? As Mrs Palli had cautioned me, no woman goes out uncovered. If tourists take photos, we ignore the intrusion. No one can see who the lady is in the picture.

Riyaz steers me by the arm to the bakery-café of his school friend, Faroukh. We hover at the entrance. It's packed in there; all the benches heaving. Faroukh clears a space for a foreigner wearing a floppy sun hat. He commands a row of teenage boys to move, and they slide into another bench, six of them hunched in a space for three. The single female tourist takes the vacated bench. Faroukh has put on his English voice. 'Don't mind the ambience,' he waves his hand at the café, 'but try our home-made snacks. You'll love them. Vegetable puff for you?'

'But I love the ambience,' she protests.

At my side, Riyaz starts laughing. I know he's going to tease Faroukh who's now calling into the kitchen: 'One sugar-less tea for the lady.'

He ambles over to us and speaks in his normal voice. 'Two days late,' he complains to Riyaz. 'You were meant to deliver the videos last week. And have tea with me.'

'There's been no time.' Riyaz hands over a USB stick. His colleague at work has been making marketing videos for Faroukh. 'Can't stop today,' he mutters. 'But, soon. I'll come for tea in a day or so.'

'There's no time here either.' Faroukh fills a plate with five different cookies. All are specialties of the house, baked on the premises. He deposits the plate at the tourist's table. Using his English accent again, he lists the flavours and tells her to try them all. She demurs. 'I'll leave the plate here. Try whatever you fancy,' he says, 'and I'll charge you just for what you consume.'

All heads have swivelled towards her but she seems unbothered. She's the only woman sitting in the café. She takes pictures on her phone, first of her little cup of tea, then the plate of biscuits, then surreptitiously she tries to capture Faroukh.

This bakery has been here for sixty years. Faroukh is the fourth generation owner. When he finished school, he went to the UK for his degree in economics. At least, I think that's what he studied. All good Indian kids who own businesses need to study economics, right? The café lies in the shadow of two ancient mosques. There is not much Faroukh can change in this old space, not that he wants to. Even his dress is the same as his ancestors, worn with more of a flourish. He wears his thick white kurta longer than the norm. His white pyjamas stop at ankle length and the plain-looking black sandals on his feet are wide-strapped designer items. His white topi was crocheted by his grandmother and is a work of art.

He returns bearing a paper packet that he gives to Riyaz.

'Coconut cookies for Sabina. I know they're her favourite.' Riyaz passes the package to me. There's already a sheen of grease on the paper. I wrap two tissues around the packet and slip it into my purse.

'I can see you're busy,' Riyaz says, meaning *I'm* busy. Later he'll tease Faroukh about his self-deprecating conversation with the foreigner, not now in front of me and the crowd at the door.

Faroukh is already back at the tourist's table, entreating the woman in his English accent to leave a review on Trip Adviser. He has a series of amazing reviews on there. She is charmed by him. I glance swiftly at her clothes. She's one of those sensible ones, a loose long-sleeved shirt, linen culottes. If she'd come in here in a skirt, she'd have had everyone staring at her legs, except Faroukh of course. Even Riyaz, who is used to women in skirts in his office, and was used to me wearing skirts, albeit long ones, when occasionally he took me out for lunch when we dated, would gaze more than he should if he saw a bare-legged woman in the old city. Context is everything.

'Be appropriate,' my mother always says. *I'm listening,* I tell her silently. Look at me. I'm about to ask Riyaz if he found the lady in the café attractive when a woman clicks by on her powder-blue heels. 'That's Marlie Auntie!' I exclaim, before he can speak.

'You're getting good at this,' Riyaz grins at me with pride.

When I first moved here, we had a ritual. I'd have to guess who the ladies around us in the market or the streets were. Everyone in a burqa and niqab.

'How do *you* recognize everyone?' I'd ask him.

'Not everyone. But most ladies, yes. See, that one. She has a long neck and stares straight ahead when she walks. That's Roop.'

Or, 'That's Shahnaz. Easy to spot. Hippo hips.'

I didn't like that and said so.

'OK, Sabina. I understand. Never explain from a man's perspective.' He was laughing. Because I knew women would also know her from her girth and her rolling gait. In time, I would guess in the same way.

I thought about my mother-in-law's walking style. Would I recognise her? Had I paid attention? Did she 'waddle like a duck', another of Riyaz's observations. Did her gloom escape her shroud and drag at her feet? Actually, no. Outside the home she walked purposefully, sensible sandals swatting the ground. Remember though, she was not on an *outing*. Never. She was doing errands. An outing for the sake of it, like I jaunt off on, would be *frivolous*.

Am I too fun-loving? It's a question I've begun to ask but there isn't really an answer. Am I to become pinched with endless cooking and dusting? Is that my future? To have plump babies and be a more docile woman?

My mother-in-law's only visits to other homes are to give condolence when acquaintances have died, suitably solemn occasions which don't require a smile. When my mother noticed that my mother-in-law couldn't smile at me, even on my wedding day, she took me aside. 'Be patient and calm to all you meet in your new home.' Well, there was only one other person in my new home other than Riyaz so I understood the reference. She added, 'You made your bed, you must lie on it.'

Ah, bed. Lying on a bed with Riyaz. That is what I'd wanted. I wanted it to be sanctioned. I wonder why approval mattered so much.

Riyaz and I hid our love. On late afternoons, he would wait some distance from the college and we would walk together by the canal, talking, before he returned to work. We did not walk hand in hand. If I touched him, if I tried to brush even the tips of his fingers, he would move away from me. 'Not here; not in public.'

He was right, but I sulked. Sometimes we passed a policewoman walking in the other direction on the canal path. She'd be carrying a striped canvas bag filled with vegetables and fruit. Riyaz would nod at her. 'That's Amna. Off-duty now. On her way home.' Her face was veiled in a khaki scarf and she wore the police uniform of khaki tunic and trousers. He'd smile indulgently at my questioning frown. 'She lives in the old town. I know her gait. I recognise her even with her face covered.' Amna would nod back politely. I felt her eyes on me, perhaps identifying me as a student. Riyaz told me that the road outside the college gates was within her patch. Occasionally I saw her too, on the road, dealing with accidents, stopping suspected criminals with her team, or on a quiet day, just sorting out the traffic jam. She never spoke to me. Riyaz said it was because she was a discreet woman and good at her job. She must see a lot that she would never talk about to anyone in the old city.

In those days, when my parents drove out of town to visit my sister and her baby, I would smuggle Riyaz into my bedroom after dark. He'd leave before dawn. Before he left, I'd mark him. Deep streaks with my nails. His shoulders, his upper back. If there was another woman, I wanted her to know about me. Riyaz would surrender to my immature clawing, even as he whispered, 'There's no need, Sabina, I tell you there's no need for this.'

One night I'd had enough. I sat at the dining table, sipping tulsi tea. I'd switched off the lights but the yellow glow from the

165

hall was enough to see the shapes of the pot, the mug, the table. The shape of Riyaz as he crept in, knelt by my chair.

'What is it?'

'I want to lie with you in *your* bed, in *your* home, *every* night.'

'My home is not like yours, Sabina. It's…different.'

'I know. I can adapt.'

'You haven't even seen my home.'

'Then show me.'

'You will change your mind.'

I know how tightly I held his face. 'How will I change my mind about you? Don't you understand anything?'

He rose and sat on a chair next to me. 'I will take you to meet my mother.'

He wasn't the only one who tried to dissuade me from marrying him. My closest friend said, 'I like him. He's a practical man. He's slightly older than us so he's wise. If Riyaz himself tells you marriage isn't a good idea, you're not going to mind me telling you. You're crazy. Stupid crazy.'

'Love-crazy?' I asked.

'That's the same as stupid-crazy. How does it make any sense for a smart, free-spirited woman to choose to live in the old city? You're used to doing as you please. You know what's going to happen.'

Love is illogical. If it was logical, it wouldn't be love. Rumi said: 'Love risks everything and asks for nothing…' But the latter part was not true of me. I risked and I made demands.

That first time I came to this house. I removed my outer layers, newly-bought, and Riyaz's mother invited me to sit by her on

166

the sofa. She looked me over carefully and at the end of the inspection, her eyes rested pointedly on my fingernails. I turned them into my palms in silence. They were clean, unvarnished. Guilt must've risen in my face. I hadn't considered that the woman who'd see the scratches I'd inflicted on Riyaz would be his mother. When? Had she noticed during the summer? In the heat-wave his abrasions had become itchy and swollen and he'd had to dab calamine lotion on them regularly. He told me he couldn't wait to take off his shirt and at home he wore only a singlet. He'd been so uncomfortable that I'd resisted with my jealous habit until the monsoon hit and he healed.

On that first visit to what would be my new home he was as nervous as I was. 'Let me show you upstairs where my room is.' He led the way.

His mother followed. She watched me as I looked around his bedroom.

'If you tell me what you want,' Riyaz said, 'I will get everything done as you like, before the marriage.'

'It's very nice.' *Lie.* 'There's no need to change anything.' *Everything would have to go.* 'I'll be just fine.' *I would do the makeover once I was installed.* I wanted to give no excuse to his mother to say an unkind word about me before the wedding. I feared that in her eyes I was wanton. I didn't know then that she would label me frivolous.

She was a woman who felt twice-betrayed by fate and who wore her misery on her sleeve. Her husband had died young. Her daughter, brought up in the old city, had rebelled against all the restrictions. She lived in Paris and visited every few years.

I knew it would be no use to quote Rumi to her: 'Escape from the black cloud that surrounds you. Then you'll see your own light as radiant as the full moon.' Young though I was, I'd begun to see that not every woman grew as wise with age as my own mother had.

Riyaz, however, was full of loyal praise for his mother. Before I'd met her he'd told me: 'My mother is an intelligent woman. She's perfectly fluent in three languages.' 'My mother is talented with her hands, she embroiders beautifully.' 'My mother is a fantastic cook.'

Not once did he say, 'She's an unhappy neurotic person who will hate you.'

Why hadn't he warned me? When he too noticed at our nikah that she couldn't smile for us, he took me aside just like my mother had done a few minutes earlier. He brought my hands up to his heart. 'I will make you happy, Sabina, I promise.'

A few weeks ago Riyaz took me to high tea at the newly restored palace of the nawab that was now a hotel. He asked his mother to accompany us.

'I've seen the palace,' she sniffed. 'I've seen it a million times. It's as dilapidated as my life.'

'You haven't been inside since it was restored,' he cajoled. 'It's only just opened. Come with us.'

'I don't like lah-di-da manners.'

'Just have a cup of masala tea there if you like,' he pleaded. 'You'll be able to point out what they've got wrong in the restoration.' Riyaz knows how to amuse her. He's a very good son.

'You go. I'll have my tea at home.'

At the palace gates, I rolled my burqa into my bag and went in on Riyaz's arm, in a floor-length dress and a gauzy scarf on my hair. Tea was served on a shady terrace. Huge butterflies flitted in the shrubs around us. The china was white and dainty. I was slightly bemused. I wanted colours and patterns, but the cups, saucers, teapots, milk jugs, everything was plain white. Even the slim white vase that held the vivid purple blooms of an orchid. Riyaz said I could take the flower out of the vase and take it home.

'Don't be silly.' But I touched it. Stroked it.

Unusually, he enjoyed the high tea more than I did. I found the cakes too creamy, too chocolatey. Riyaz gorged on the open cucumber sandwiches. He ate both our portions of scones with clotted cream and rose-petal jam.

I remember he'd so relished the tea that he'd told the waiter, 'We're definitely coming back.' I didn't realise I was gazing into the distance as I walked.

'You're dreaming about food, aren't you?' Sometimes Riyaz guesses what I'm thinking. 'Shall we go back to the palace hotel for their Nawabi dinner for our anniversary?' He stops for a moment at the Bangle Bazaar junction. 'Thirteen courses, remember that mouthwatering menu?' He touches my elbow. 'Let's not think about how many thousand rupees it costs. That's what you're dreaming of, right?'

Wrong. Although food is part of the Goa dream if I take into account the prawn curry. I stay silent. He walks on. 'I'll need to eat something quick. I must return to the office soon. What should we share, Sabina?'

'Nothing. I don't want to eat. I'm not hungry.' My stomach clenches in disbelief at my words.

He stops again. 'You must eat lunch.'

'Don't tell me what to do. Do *not* tell me what I *must* do.'

'You told me you would adjust, remember? You insisted that you could-'

'*Don't* remind me of my mistakes.' I place my hand on his cheek. It lands as a light slap. Half-joking, half-meant. My anger has bubbled out suddenly, taking me by surprise.

We hear a camera click. A tourist has snapped the moment. Riyaz looks at her, she's a few feet away on a side street, under a shady awning. His face darkens. 'You shame me in public, *begum.*' He crosses the road to a biryani stall, leaving me standing alone. I wait. He returns holding a paper plate heaped with vegetable rice. He begins to eat, motioning to a spare fork.

'Eat.'

'No.'

I know how I punish him. He deserves it. He would hop off to his office. I would return to an afternoon of my mother-in-law's complaints. My life of restraints.

We part at the next crossroads. I watch him for a few moments, tenderness and anger roiling in my heart. I realise he's not heading out of the old city. I call to him, he turns.

'Why are you going that way?'

He walks back. 'I'm going to the flower stall. I want to see if he has anything interesting today.'

He can tell I'm beaming even though my face is veiled.

One evening last week we retired upstairs to our bedroom early. When I snuggled up to him, he withdrew a carefully wrapped flower from his jacket pocket. A purple orchid. He didn't hand it to me though. When I was half undressed and lying on the bed, he placed it between my breasts, sliding the stem under my bra at the front. 'Keep your bra on.'

He kissed the contours of my bra and the outline of the flower.

Before he settled to sleep for the night he plucked the orchid from me and slid it under his pillow.

I wonder what flower he'll find today. Will I be as pleased if it's just a common marigold? How would that look between my breasts?

I quicken my pace. Daydreaming and dawdling are frivolous activities. I almost bump into the woman walking ahead of me. She's in a thick cotton burqa. I recognise the blue stripy bag stuffed with groceries. Half-day, Amna? I think. You're home early. I slow down to walk behind her. All this time, she's been under my nose and I've taken her for granted. She crosses the invisible barriers of these lanes each day. Somewhere on the fringe of the old city there must be a spot where the auto-rickshaw drops off Amna and she slips on her outer garments before proceeding home. Does she hastily pin the niqab over her khaki scarf? Aren't you overheated and stifling, Amna? No. She walks coolly wherever she is.

I'm reminded of Amna's beat and where I want to be. Would I be fulfilled then, at the women's college? I have Riyaz, I have marriage and a home with him, what if I had academia too? If I followed the rules like Amna did, could I live a dual life: inside and outside the old city? Would my resentments towards my husband dissolve?

I'd have to bear the barbs, that's all. If Amna could, I could. Like the proverb states: Sticks and stones may break my bones but words will never hurt me.

Once home I hurry up the stairs to my bedroom. My mother-in-law is already calling from the kitchen. I'm starving but I can't go down and scoff something straightaway. How to explain why I didn't eat with Riyaz? I'll have to wait till five, till tea. I delve in my bag for the packet from Faroukh. Those delectable coconut cookies crumble in my mouth; they'll have to keep me going.

I rummage in my cupboard to find the bra I'm looking for. In the early evening I'll wash off the dust of the day and change my undergarments. I'll wear something lacy this evening, something to take Riyaz's breath away.

If I get time to myself before he comes home and before we have dinner, I'll start the PhD application on my laptop. I may not mention it to him until later though. Maybe when he's very relaxed and about to sleep. I'll tell him about the second phone call from Mrs Palli and her invitation to return to philosophy.

A MEDITERRANEAN SUMMER

Reshma Ruia

The first time he touched it
The sea
His hand drew back
Frightened Excited
His skin could not understand the language
Of something so slippery shiny and pure
Eight days and nights he walked
Barefoot beneath the Sun
At night his head pillowed on desert sand
He dreamt of rain-a feathered claw stroking his cheek
The day arrives
The rubber dinghy growls impatient
He smells petrol fumes He smells fear
Of a hundred bodies pressing near
Closed fists holding tight their world
Razor blade voices shout
He cowers afraid as the dinghy

Shudders awake
Trailing his fingers in the water…aah
The wine dark sea
And he weeps for what he has left behind
For what lies ahead
The orange jacket floats aimlessly skimming water
A stray sandal and soggy blanket
Postcards from an unfinished voyage
'A minor inconvenience' the waiter murmurs
Tilting beach umbrellas block the view
Champagne shimmers in the noonday Sun
Well-fed bodies arch their backs
Fiddle with their IPhone
The DJ's beat drowns out the sighs
Of those sinking out of sight
Platters of fruit lie uneaten
Models strut their wares
Pouting lips and sulky eyes
'It's good to be alive' smirks the Oligarch to his wife
It is just another summer on the Mediterranean

SONNY

CG Menon

Sonny's new flat was a spidery, fifth-floor ribbon of glass. Out of the window I could see Canary Wharf across the water with its spangled office towers and windows blank as newsprint. My cousin ate his cornflakes to the glow of Citibank, watched TV by the light of J.P. Morgan, and had nightly sex sponsored by Barclays. He stood at the window with a conscious, bored kick to his hips. *Like the view, Mohan?* his cocked head asked. I looked away.

'What's all this stuff?' I asked. There were boxes that didn't belong to him, shoe carriers and tatty, trinky ornaments. An Orla Kiely make-up bag thrown on top. And a prayer rug, laid out on the floor with its edges sharp as a ruler.

He shrugged. 'It's all Kaya's. She moved some of her things in on Saturday.'

I could feel his glow when he came close, those rounded cheeks stained like rose-leaves and his red lips sticky with gin. Skin-deep succulent, that was Sonny, because under all that sugar was a taste like a burnt match.

The front door slammed. Naz had been finishing off his

cigarette outside and annoying Sonny's neighbours. Causing trouble, without saying a word. He flicked me on the temple with a yellow-nailed finger and pushed past to the narrow kitchen. Seemed like he knew his way around Sonny's flat better than I did.

'A prayer rug, eh?' he called. Sonny rolled his eyes. He didn't like Naz either, I sometimes thought. But he did want to be him.

'On her knees five times a day?' Naz was sneering now, his voice curdling over the sounds of a bottle being opened. 'Well get *you*, Sonny lad.'

'Shut it, Naz. She doesn't use the mat anyway. It's *cultural*.' Sonny wrapped his mouth around the word, tasting it. His eyes shifted as though he were apologising. Making excuses for Kaya, for the rug and her dainty little boots by the door. For the boxes stuffed with copies of Cosmo and draped with jewellery.

'Does Uncle know? About Kaya?' I asked him quietly.

He looked away, shrugged. 'Leave it out, Mohan. It'll be fine.'

Naz walked back into the room with three whiskies dribbled into sticky glasses.

'Hey, Mo.' He licked his lips. 'You going to fix young Sonny up when Lehman goes bust? Flog his arse down Soho to all your rice queen lov-airs so he can keep paying for that Muslim pussy?'

Naz was a thug, Home Counties in a Paul Smith suit. He called in sick every Friday, Sonny said, and spent Instagrammed hours at the Lehman gym instead of his desk. I'd looked up his page: Naz grunting over the squat rack, Naz gulping a mix of protein powder, Naz flexing and in love with his own reflection. I knew the pictures off by heart, one hand on the mouse and one around my cock.

Naz looked at us, a flickering, sizing-you-up glance and draped his arm over Sonny's shoulder. I felt sick suddenly, felt bile drop and swell in my stomach and I fled to the white-tiled bathroom.

The next day Sonny and I met in Greenwich. The café was crowded, its enamel tables squashed into a pavement space that wasn't really big enough. I hunched, with my elbows and knees tucked tight as a ready-roast chicken. Sonny spread his legs, straddled forward, and wiped his tongue around the salt on his glass.

'Sonny …you said Kaya was moving in.'

He didn't reply, just turned round to face me and took another gulp.

'Man, are you serious? Really?'

He tipped his sunglasses towards his nose, then shoved them back, placid as a cat.

'Take those fucking glasses off, Sonny. Why didn't you tell me?'

He pulled the frames away and I saw his forehead glisten. Sonny was always sweating, some kind of perspiration problem that made him glossy as a toffee-apple and left damp handprints on everything he touched. He examined his nailbeds, brushing my question off. 'She's just staying for a bit, not forever. It can't hurt, Mo.'

Sonny always thought things couldn't hurt.

'Your dad will go mental.' There was no other word for it. Apan-uncle was built like a wrestler and talked like a Hindu nationalist. He'd come over from India forty years ago with Asha-auntie and had regretted it ever since. He still thought he'd arrange Sonny's marriage one day. He'd import some fair-skinned distant cousin from Delhi with an MBA and a fresh-scrubbed womb. Desi girls only. No Westerners. No sluts. Definitely, definitely no Muslims. Kaya wasn't exactly fundamentalist – she smoked and drank and, according to Sonny, could suck the lead from a pencil – but somehow I didn't think that would make Apan-uncle any happier.

I'd seen a lot of Apan-uncle and Asha-auntie a few years ago. After I'd graduated from Imperial, my parents left to go back home. Uncle Apan invited me to his house, clapped me heavily on the back. *Look at this boy, doctor-in-training, eh.*

And then I'd come out.

The invitations had dried up after that. Apan-uncle stopped slapping my back, and started holding his hands behind his own. Talking about incest, moral corruption, boys-who-think-they're-girls, and Sonny hadn't said a word.

'It's all right, Mo.' His words broke in on my thoughts, pulling me back to the café with its sticky tables. 'Dad doesn't want to know. Not about Kaya.'

Next to us a couple were gathering their things together. Packing up like a couple of Kensington Sherpas loaded with baby paraphernalia, sunglasses and designer bags. They left a litter of sticky glasses spilled across the table and a Guardian folded messily at the property supplement. 'Shares drop as Lehman totters,' blared the next page.

'Sonny?' He was staring at the newspaper, flexing his fingers again and again on his empty glass.

'Another drink?' I offered.

He pushed his glasses up, rumpling his hair and smiled at me for the first time that day.

'It'll be all right, Mo,' he said quietly. He jerked his thumb at the paper and his voice rose slightly, trembling into a question. 'Always exaggerate these things, don't they?'

He trailed off there, and didn't say another word. The drinks came, along with some coins from the change. As I reached out he put his hand over mine. His nails were stubby half-crescents curved like yellow beaks over his fingertips. After a second, a heartbeat, I slid my hand away and left the coins in his palm.

I'd known Sonny since we were both tiny. My parents used to visit Apan-uncle and Asha-auntie for weekends. I'd be tucked into the spare-room bed with Sonny. We'd squabble together, hitting and snuffling in the stifling cavern of Auntie's second-best duvet, both of us with a torch or Lego figurine jammed in our fat little fists. Sonny's family lived in Whitechapel, in a maisonette that smelt of stale turmeric and hair-oil. My parents always brought over a gift, some vases or a few cellophane-wrapped shirts.

Don't be silly, Apan, eh? My father's voice would float in through the spare-room door. *All between brothers, money's no object.*

Last year Sonny had bought his parents a new place in Earl's Court – all that Lehman money had to be spent somewhere – but the turmeric and hair-oil smell moved with them. Asha-Auntie never really settled in, and it was only a few weeks after the move that her Alzheimer's diagnosis came through. Fucking *mad*, Sonny burst out in the doctor's office, and Apan-uncle moved to hit him before slumping back in tears. Now she sat at home all day with a blanket folded under her hips. She was still lovely, soft and pillowy with a glazed unfocussed smile but she'd forgotten how to speak anything but Hindi.

I didn't visit much anymore, not since Sonny told me Apan-uncle hosed the toilet down with bleach each time I left. He'd snorted with laughter, a braying gulp just like Naz's, as though he were choking on his own spit. If I hadn't loved him, I'd have wanted to hit him too.

'Hold on a sec, Mo, let me text her.' It was eight o'clock, it was Saturday night and Kaya still hadn't arrived at the bar. Sonny couldn't settle.

'You were half an hour late yourself, man,' I reminded him.

'Yeah, well, she doesn't know that, does she? It's fucking disrespectful.'

It wasn't like Sonny to be on edge, but nothing had been normal the last few days. He hadn't mentioned work – not even when Barclays had sacked half their brokers two days ago – and somehow I couldn't ask him either. He used to be glued to his phone, used to swipe down to the stock market section with the same expression as he watched Kaya when she was getting drunk. Anticipatory.

We were in a wine bar in Hoxton, a chilly place with retro silk shades over the lights and slippery red stools. It was half-full and there was a loud clatter of cocktail shakers and the occasional hiss of steam from the kitchen, but nobody was talking.

When the door slammed back I knew it was Naz. Nobody else walked into a room that way. He shouldered his way through the sparse crowd like they were Oxford Street Christmas shoppers and I felt my stomach sink. Kaya trailed after him, her eyelids pink and her lipstick smudged. She'd been crying, or trying not to.

Sonny didn't notice. 'Hey, sexy! Thought you weren't going to turn up.'

Kaya looked just like Sonny's other girls, with her manicured nails and strappy sandals and a huge handbag balanced on one skinny wrist. No headscarf. Girls like Kaya wouldn't dream of wearing them. He gave her a kiss, a long, open-mouthed one, and she sniffed, wriggled her shoulders back and pulled her skirt down. She was lovely, even I could tell that, but Naz was right about one thing. Kaya wouldn't come cheap.

'Naz and I were chatting.' She shot him a filthy look.

'Can I talk to you a moment, Sonny?' Without looking at me, she walked straight past and into a booth. Sonny shrugged and followed her.

'All right, my man?' Naz and I were marooned in a puddle of light, watching the reflections of the lampshades dip and sway on the polished bar.

I nodded. 'What did you say to Kaya?'

'Oh, nothing, nothing.' He was flipping the top of a beer bottle up and catching it on his hand. 'We used to play this at school. Jacks. Did you play it too, Mo?'

'What?'

'Needs slippery fingers, doesn't it? Thought you'd be good at it.' He had a little smile that creased his lips, a dirty little grin that slipped out for a second as he looked me up and down.

'What are you on about, Naz? What's your probl – '

I stopped as Kaya barged out of the booth. She pushed past us both in a wind of scent, her coat flapping open and her bag slung over her wrist. She jerked open the door and disappeared outside. Now she was crying.

I felt a touch on my shoulder and turned to see Sonny. He gave a lopsided shrug, a little half-hearted and awkward nod.

'Do me a favour, Mo. Go after her. Get her to come back in and talk properly.'

I'd never refused Sonny a favour, not when he smiled at me like that.

The door was stiff, and as soon as I'd got it open it slammed behind me with the wind from a passing bus. The bar was on a main road, an inflamed stripe of headlamps and traffic lights.

Kaya hadn't gone far. She was leaning against the slippery seat of a bus shelter with the notice board flickering orange light over her hair.

'Kaya?'

Perhaps she'd been hoping Sonny would follow her, because when she heard my voice her head snapped up.

'Fuck you!' she spat. 'Get away from me.'

I stopped by the smeared glass of the bus stop. Looking at myself, all transparent and washed out. As though I were hardly there at all.

'I wouldn't touch him now,' she muttered without looking up. 'I didn't know he was like that. He's all yours, Mo.'

'Kaya, what are you…'

Her head dropped and she started to cry again.

'Look, just come back in. Sonny wants you. Come on, Kaya…'

I sat down next to her on the bus seat and put my hand on her arm. It was warm and damp, and she shivered like a cat being stroked.

'Mo – stop it. Stop…' she took a deep breath. 'Naz said you and Sonny used to… do stuff. Together.'

God, Naz. What the fuck had he said?

'Stuff? You mean like…' Praying she meant something innocuous. Shoplifting, maybe, or coke. Armed robbery.

'Sex stuff. Naz says Sonny's a fag.' The word slapped out of her mouth. Then she grabbed at my hand, held it tight. God, she was a mess, all over the place, but I could hardly blame her. 'I'm sorry, Mo. I'm sorry. I'm just worried…what if he's got something? He ought to have told me. I've got a right to know.'

Kaya was a sweetie, even sniffing back tears, even wiping her nose on the back of her hand and asking if I've given Sonny AIDS. She was his type, no doubt about it, all huge eyes and apologies and for a second I could have gutted Naz for whatever he'd said. But Sonny must have told him first.

A spare room, in Apan-uncle and Asha-auntie's house. A duvet smelling of mothballs. Both of us just a shade too old to share a bed any more. Voices floating from the living room. *Take the money, Apan, we all help each other out.* Helping each other out. Brothers. Family together, and Sonny's hand on me in what could almost be one of those play-fights we'd outgrown. Almost.

Damp handprints on everything he touched, that was Sonny, and sometimes they never scrubbed off.

Kaya was sniffing, burrowing through her huge handbag for a tissue and combing her fingers through her hair. She wasn't saying any more, at least for now. Through the shade-fringed window of the bar I could see Sonny. He'd dropped one arm round Naz's broad shoulders. He was laughing – that gutteral laugh, snorting in his throat – and he clapped Naz on the back. Congratulations, Sonny, I thought. Apan-uncle all over again. I wondered if Sonny bleached the bathroom after I left, too. I wondered if everything had been a joke, with him. Something you laughed about with your mates. Something he thought wouldn't hurt.

'Kaya...' She was getting to her feet, pigeon-toed in those strappy sandals that must have hurt. A bus pulled up, puddling light out. A noise, a stench of something unwashed and homeless.

'So, did you? Mo?' she asked. 'Did you fuck him? Or did he fuck you?'

'Kaya!' For a second I could have hit her, lovely though she was. 'Look, do you think it matters?'

She looked at me, and Sonny's laugh was thudding through my head somewhere deeper than hearing. 'Sonny's not sticking with you anymore than with me. He's not...'

I stopped talking. I wanted to tell Kaya she was just a shag, for Sonny. At least I was a dirty little secret.

She blinked, as though she hadn't heard me or couldn't quite believe what I'd said. When I leant closer, she stepped back and pulled her face into her neck. It gave her a brief double-chin, a few turtling rings around her neck where the glaring light bounced off pools of flesh.

'What?' Her voice was quiet.

I shrugged. 'He laughed at your prayer mat, didn't he? Wants you on your knees but that's about as far as he'll go.'

It was Naz's joke, that one about her knees. He owed me that much.

Kaya didn't answer. She leant down and adjusted the strap of her sandals, then slung her bag onto her shoulder and clipped off down the street. At the next bus-stop she paused, looked back for a second, then jerked her thumb for a taxi. She was heartbreaking, Kaya, climbing into that black cab with her hair swinging and her legs smooth as glass. She was too good for Sonny. Too good for me or Naz. Too good for anything at all.

My phone rang a few hours later. I'd been walking non-stop, crossing bridges and roads and wandering through blank-faced parking lots.

'Sonny.' It was Asha-auntie. 'Sonny', she said, again and again, and all the rest of it in Hindi I couldn't understand.

'Auntie... it's Mo. Mo.' I held the phone against my ear for a second, me and Asha-auntie saying things to each other that didn't make sense and never would. It wasn't me that she wanted, but I thought perhaps she couldn't even tell. Eventually I left the call open and pushed the phone into my back pocket. I walked for the rest of the night. I could have called Sonny, I suppose, but I wouldn't have known what to say.

Sonny was head-hunted by Goldman Sachs within a week of the Lehman collapse. He didn't shamble out with a cardboard box in his arms and a thousand camera flashes in his eyes, or leap in front of the Northern line at some grimy and irrelevant tube stop. Instead, he watched it all happen from a small TV by his mother's hospital bedside. Asha-auntie had had a stroke on Saturday night, and had been admitted to hospital. Sonny hadn't known until Sunday morning, by which time she'd long since stopped asking for him. Sonny had sat there all night, Apan-uncle told me, holding his mother's hand until it was too late for anything else.

I saw Sonny again yesterday, quite by chance. He was in the vodka bar in Greenwich, his fat rose-leaf cheeks bulging with oysters and gin. There was a girl sitting opposite him, laughing. She had poker-straight hair and French-tipped nails, another Kaya down to her strappy red shoes.

I wanted to ask him if it was worth it, any of it. I wanted to ask if Naz still wore a Paul Smith suit and if Kaya ever came back. I wanted to ask if she'd taken her prayer mat and if it had done her any good. I wanted to ask if he remembered the spare room and if his hands still sweated at night. But I didn't. Some things can't hurt, I suppose, but I never learnt to say them.

LIVING WITH THE DEAD

Nadia Kabir Barb

I often think about death. It used to lurk in the deep recesses of my mind but these days it pops up like a Jack-in-the-box with an annoying frequency. The preoccupation has long ceased to be a fear of dying and over time evolved into an acceptance of the inevitable. The only questions that remain are how and when? I suppose sitting in a cemetery might have something to do with it.

I wasn't always this morbid or reclusive. Being surrounded by family and friends was something I enjoyed. Or maybe I just thought I did. The desire for solitude crept up on me and before I knew it I was spending my free time alone perhaps because there was already enough noise inside my head. I needed peace and quiet. Time to think. Time to just be. There's something quite liberating about sitting under the great expanse of open sky with the dead as my companions. I've become acquainted with many of the residents within the walls and my imagination has filled in the blanks: who they were, how they lived and how they died.

A couple walk past me carrying a small bunch of flowers. I

shift my weight on the bench to watch where they'll stop. It's one of the newer graves.

I run my fingers along the green peeling paint of the wooden seat. Feels like being reacquainted with an old friend. It's been a while since I was last here. The bolt-like nail on the right-hand side is still jutting out. I reach out and touch it. The memories are as fresh as if it were yesterday. I can hear our voices in our silent surroundings.

'I think I want to be cremated,' I said quietly, while watching Leo smudge charcoal on the paper with his finger.

He looked up. 'Aren't you Muslim?'

I nodded.

'I thought you had to be buried.'

'Yes, we do. I guess if I were in Bangladesh, it might be an issue. In fact, it would definitely be an issue but I'm here, so I hope my family will respect my wishes. Plus, I'm claustrophobic. Don't like the thought of being covered by soil.' I shuddered involuntarily. 'With worms and bugs as my eternal companions? I don't think so.'

He stopped drawing and looked at me. 'I doubt you'll really care at that point, you know with the being dead and all.' He was laughing at me.

'I didn't say it was a rational thought, just a preference.'

I rolled my eyes at him but he'd disappeared back into his sketchpad. I tried to look at his drawing which he guarded with an uncharacteristic possessiveness.

'What about you? Do you want to be buried, cremated…?'

'Me? Don't care. When I'm dead, my body's just a carcass. Makes no difference to me if I'm buried or cremated or left in

188

a ditch to rot.' Somehow his response didn't surprise me.

'Rotting corpses in ditches aren't particularly great for the environment. You know, with the stench and all...plus you'd have to travel to the countryside to find a ditch. I don't think London is a ditch-rich area.'

He glanced at me and laughed. 'Point taken. OK, maybe not a ditch. But don't you think that how or when we die should be a choice? There's so much of my life I didn't get to choose. Wouldn't it be empowering to have control over our death?'

I knew he wasn't joking. We'd danced around this topic a few times in previous conversations. His father had left his mother when she had been pregnant with him. He'd never even met the man. Years of dealing with a single parent suffering from depression had left him cynical about what life had to offer. It wasn't the life he'd chosen but had been imposed upon him. That was how he saw it.

'Choosing the time or the way you die is...well what you're talking about is suicide. I'm not sure I agree. I think some things have to be left to chance or fate or whatever you want to call it.'

'So conventional of you, Bina.'

I didn't mind the comment so much as the accompanying look of disappointment.

He stood up suddenly. 'Let's walk.'

I got up and fell in step with him. The cemetery was empty as usual. Over time we realised we were the only regular visitors. A world apart from the graveyard where my grandmother was buried in Dhaka. I remember the blanket of heat that engulfed me and the heady fragrance of jasmine in the air. That too was a resting place for the dead, but it hummed continuously with the sound and movement of people paying their respects to the departed. It was a place for peaceful contemplation but not solitude. I told Leo that those who were buried there never wanted for company with rows and rows of graves lined up next to each other.

'Aww look, Maisy Duck's had a visitor,' I said, pointing at a large gravestone with a small posy of roses. We had fallen in love with the name and she'd become one of our favourites.

'About time. What's the point of all this?' he said pointing to the graves surrounding us. 'Fancy headstones, elaborate epitaphs. Who the hell is even going to remember or come and visit in a few years? Ashes to ashes, dust to dust…'

'Oh for God's sake stop being so bloody morose. I thought this place allowed you to think and meditate.'

He stopped and turned to face me. 'Are all Bangladeshi women as fierce as you?' He was smiling. 'I was going to give this to you later but let's call it a peace offering.' He handed me the drawing he'd been working on. The woman in the sketch was undeniably me. The cheekbones, the mouth, the eyes, the hair, but it was not any me that I'd ever imagined. The lines were dark and bold, the shading deep, the angles sharp, almost exaggerated, and the contrast pronounced. It was uncharacteristic even for Leo's highly stylised sketches. And the face was beautiful. So this was how he saw me.

Before I had a chance to say anything, he bent his head and his lips covered mine. For a second, I allowed myself to yield to the pressure of his mouth and then guilt made me pull away. It felt like we were being disrespectful to the dead. Now I wish I could return to that moment and give in to my feelings.

I first met Leo in the cemetery. We shared the view that the dead are far more accommodating and peaceful than the living. I suppose that was what brought us together in the first place, a respite from the emotional cacophony that accompanies us like a constant, unwanted companion. Life with the living can be a draining experience.

At the end of Spring almost two years earlier, I had agreed to attend a photography exhibition organised by Janet, an old friend from school. It was at the Dissenter's Gallery which is adjacent to the chapel in our local cemetery. Odd place for an exhibition I thought, but went along to show my support.

I arrived early and because it was an unusually mild and balmy evening, I wandered around the cemetery while I waited for the exhibition room to open. The first thing I noticed was the silence. It was as if even the birds had stopped chirping out of respect for the dead. I wondered why people spoke in hushed tones in a graveyard. It wasn't as if any of the inhabitants would be disturbed by the noise. The quietness seeped into my body and I felt at peace. I sat down on a bench and looked at the assortment of tombstones. A homage to the people who have moved on from the people left behind.

A couple of weeks later, on my way back from work, I drove past the cemetery and for reasons I still can't fathom, parked my car and walked in. Almost immediately a sense of tranquility washed over me. This time I stopped to read some of the epitaphs on the headstones:

Leslie Barker 1967 – 2002, Gone but Not Forgotten,

Mark Cummins 1863 – 1940, Beloved Husband and Father,

It was the inscriptions for the children that saddened me.

Jennifer Mathews 1901 – 1909, Our Angel Who Watches Over Us from Heaven.

I wondered how you could recover from the loss of a child.

I found myself returning every week to soak up the calming energy. I would walk through the grounds or sit on the wooden green bench and read.

On my fourth visit, as I sat reading, a man walked over and without a word parked himself on the bench. It wasn't my private property so he didn't need to ask if he could sit down but it irritated me. He barely even looked my way. Instead, he took out a notepad and a few charcoal pencils and started scribbling. I watched from the corner of my eye. He was wearing jeans and a black t-shirt. His wavy hair was in need of a trim, as was his beard, and the black rimmed glasses were thick and heavy on his face. He caught me staring at him and I could feel the blood rushing to my cheeks. I tried to look nonchalant, got up and then left.

After our first encounter, every time I visited the cemetery he seemed to be sitting on the bench, pad of paper and pencils in hand. He'd encroached on my patch of peace and quiet and hijacked it. For a while I made a point of walking past or ignoring him. I'm not sure if he even noticed but it gave me a sense of satisfaction.

It got to the stage where I expected the bearded man to be in the cemetery and one day decided to stake my claim. The bench was a little ahead of me and I made my way over and sat down. He didn't look up.

'Stalking is an offence you know?'

At first, I wasn't sure I'd heard correctly but he turned his head and was looking at me.

'What? I'm not stalk...' I trailed off. He was smiling. The man had a warped sense of humour. I gave him a perfunctory smile.

'It's a great place to think...and draw. Or read,' he said, pointing at my book.

I nodded my head.

We sat in silence and I wondered if I should introduce myself but before I had a chance, he got up.

'Enjoy,' he said, gesturing to the grounds and walked towards the exit. Strange man.

I sat for a bit longer, finished a chapter of my book and then took some photos of the changing sky on my phone. They turned out rather well.

I returned the following week. The man was sitting on the bench drawing. I think a part of me was secretly pleased.

'Hello again,' I said.

He gazed at me through his glasses and for a moment I thought there was a blank look on his face. I felt like an idiot.

'Hello you. Following me again?'

'Obviously,' I replied.

'Leo,' he said offering me his hand. I reached out and shook it. There was charcoal dust on his fingertips. 'You should at least know the name of the person you're stalking.'

'And you should know the name of your alleged stalker. Bina.' I smiled as I sat down on the bench.

Our chance encounters became a regular occurrence and we met other every week at the green bench. We grew familiar with the names of people buried and would often place a flower on those graves that had been long forgotten. We learned about each other. He was a graphics arts designer but liked to sketch in his spare time. He said he would never have guessed I was a school librarian. I never thought to ask what he meant.

During the winter, we stopped going to the cemetery and met at the local café. It wasn't the same. Too many people, too much noise. Spring saw us back at the cemetery, at our green bench. The last time I met him, he gave me the portrait.

Leo died a year ago. His family buried him. Not here, but in a quiet little cemetery with manicured gardens in North London. They say he didn't see the oncoming bus as he stepped off the pavement. I'm not sure I believe that. I think he chose his 'how and when'. I visited his grave a few times but he was right. It felt like only his 'carcass' was lying in the casket under the ground. His essence is here. I can feel it when I walk the familiar paths flanked by the graves of people who were the silent observers in our relationship. If one can call it that. Every day I live with the burden of 'if only'. If only I'd done something to stop him. If only I'd told him how I felt. If only I'd been enough. I wonder if he's sitting on the bench next to me now, watching me and smiling as I run my finger across the peeling green paint.

First published in Bengal Lights journal 2017

INBETWEEN

Radhika Kapur

I sat cross-legged on my bed in my dark, cool bedroom, eyes shut and palms resting on my knees. I tuned into the comforting whirr of the overhead fan as I meditated. The first time I returned to Delhi from London, I turned on the fan, and suddenly realised how glad I was to hear it. A strange thing to miss – that and the sweet cooing of the Koyal bird on a balmy evening

When you meditate, the pause between two breaths is the gateway to self-realisation. Focusing on this pause is one of 112 meditation techniques that can be found in the ancient scriptural text Vigyan Bhairava.

In my meditation practice, I have often tried to focus on this elusive space. I have tried to capture it in the net of my awareness but, like a glittering fish, it wiggles and escapes, swimming away, leaving me staring at its flashing tail. There have been occasional moments when I've thought, 'There it is! I have it!' and have tried to expand the moment only to have my breath whoosh out because I have held it too long. At other times, a velvety indigo calm wraps around me as I observe my breath filling my chest, then emptying it.

I have imagined this gap as the space where dazzling fireworks will illuminate my inner sky and I will realise my oneness with the vast universe, the unending carpet of blue stretching out above, below and on every side of me. I have anticipated it as the moment in which the drop will splash into the waves, forget its smallness and become the roaring, rolling ocean. If only I can grasp it.

In 2014, I found myself plunged into a different kind of inbetween space.

I married my husband and moved to London for us to begin our lives together. Little did I know I was bungee jumping into an unknown chasm. The old me disappeared. I left her behind in Delhi. The new me was still to emerge. And, here I was, careening head-down, hands flailing into the gap between. I was, to put it simply, terrified.

Words. Words were slipping away. Words I used to describe myself. I couldn't hold onto their wet and soapy curves. 'Independent', 'financially self-sufficient' and 'career woman' were some. The rituals and routines of everyday life through which I knew myself went too: the ten to whatever time workday, getting in to the advertising agency I worked for, racing to meet deadlines, sharing *dabba* lunch with colleagues with the smell of turmeric, ginger and spices wafting into the air, the restaurants where I dined, the shop windows I pressed my nose against and the doctor's waiting room I'd sat in, waiting for my turn, since I was a child, a token number pressed into my hand. The family and friends who filled my life were no longer around me. I started searching for new words to describe who I was. I would try them out like clothes in a shop. What did I do? Was I still a copywriter? Without a job? Was I an author? Could I be an author without being published? Was I brave? Was I a failure? Was I shy? What did my new friends tell me about myself? What was my routine? My favourite new restaurant? Who was I? I was seeking. Seeking new definitions of myself.

I would look enviously at people who seemed so sure about who they were while the sands of certainty had shifted below my feet. I knew a new Radhika would come into view, but she wasn't here yet.

I had always thought of the 'gap between' as the nothingness that contains everything. I was the one who had greedily tried to clasp this nothingness to my chest time and again when I meditated, but I was shocked at how scary it felt when I actually experienced it. I should be in bliss, I thought. Why wasn't I?

The difference between my idea of this interspace and its reality made me uncomfortable. However, I believed firmly in its value. I reminded myself that I was being given the opportunity for reinvention, the chance to actually plunge my hand into nothingness and pull out a different me.

Perhaps, even before that, I was being given the chance to be comfortable with being, just being, without being something. And, that is the most daunting ask. It's so contrary to our lifelong training – to achieve, to do and to keep moving. In all this movement, it is easy to forget how to be still. The space between two selves, or two anythings for that matter, is about being confidently motionless. Often I centre my awareness on breathing. That helps.

Along the way, I turned to writing. Words helped me settle into stillness. I wrote all the things I've always wanted to write but never had the time or the kind of creative support I now found in London: a blog, short stories and screenplays. I joined writing groups, entered competitions, and took courses. When words went, I held onto the whole damn dictionary.

After years of writing in the voice of various brands, it was dizzyingly liberating to write in my own. I didn't have to sing out of the mouth of a cola bottle, the hood of a gleaming automobile or the flip-open cap of an elegant shampoo. I crept out from under the label and popped my head into the sunshine. As I wrote, I discovered my own narrative voice. I found I wrote comedy again and again. It's hard to describe the sense of wonder that accompanies such a realisation. It's like being introduced to another part of you. I sensed a new Radhika emerging and it was very, very exciting. Along the way, there have been many moments when I have been overcome with panic. There still are. Moments in which I bemoan everything I have lost. I know how powerful stories are. Yet it took a family member to sit me down and suggest I be mindful of the words I was using to describe my transition experience. To celebrate instead of complain. To shift my attitude. To embrace the opportunity to experiment. And all of a sudden my empty time felt like a gift.

I haven't meditated on the gap between breaths or thoughts for a while. Perhaps I didn't have the courage to step into that space. To lose myself. But the other day, I did. And I couldn't do it the old way, sitting there, trying to 'spot the space' like I was playing a game. My meditation practice supported my exploration of a new life stage and that in turn gave me deeper insight into my practice. I know now it's not about pouncing on that moment of pause. It's about becoming still enough for it to find you. So, that's what I focus on.

A LAUGHING MATTER

Shibani Lal

'HelloGoodMorningSir! Myself Elvis.'

'Huh?' I squinted at the blurry shapes at the door.

'GoodMorningSir!' he repeated with enthusiasm. 'Driver Elvis. Mr. Gaurav send me.'

'Ah yes!' I reached for my glasses. 'Hang on, Gaurav told me he was sending only one Driver, not two?'

'He sending me only! This...' Elvis beamed at the fellow behind him, '...my brother. Hardworking. Good cook also.'

'I don't need a cook,' I began, my voice firm. 'Only a driver. Someone who comes on time, can work late nights, you understand?'

'Yessir! Understanding! I come earlys and doing late duty also. I bring brother for just-in-cases-situations. Like if I falling sick, brother come in my place.' He coughed as though to illustrate the point. 'He live with me, there,' he continued, pointing vaguely in the direction of the sea.

The cook-brother offered me an ingratiating smile.

'To be clear, you're looking for the job, yes, not your brother?'

'Yessir. I looking job. Mr. Gaurav say you from London and...'

'You drive an Automatic?'

'Best it is for Bombay traffic! Yes! I driving all. Automatics. Manuals. Wintage. Everytypes. Here, license.'

'Vintage?'

'Wintage, yes. Buick-Bendley-Rolls-Royce-alltypes. Old Boss having many. He teach me to drive. Then he go off, and daughters sell cars.' He gave a pitiful shake of his head.

I studied his licence. 'Go off?'

His eyes widened like plums. He drew a finger across his neck and finished with a menacing cluck of his tongue.

'Oh, he died. Sorry.'

'Jejuz bless him,' said Elvis.

'Amen,' chimed the brother.

I'd been in Bombay two months, and was ready to call it a day and head back to the relative sanity of my flat on King's Road. My London home was my get out of jail free card, in case Bombay didn't work out. With each passing day, I was convinced I'd screwed up big time by coming here.

'You haven't. Give yourself a break,' my sister had said the previous evening. 'Jeez. You're so hard on yourself.'

'Di, I seem to spend all my time interviewing drivers and haggling over the equivalent of pennies. For everything!'

'It may be pennies to you, but that's a lot of money for people here. And what did you think? You'd waltz back here and poof?' she snapped her fingers. 'In the real world...'

'London's pretty real to me.'

'You've forgotten. When you first moved there you whined for ages. I remember...'

'Lies. I settled in immediately, it was...'

'Milk is tasteless, bananas aren't soft…,' she began counting on her fingers. 'No mixed taps, bloody mushrooms sprouting on the carpet in the bathroom…'

'That's unfair. I was eighteen.'

'And now you're trying to settle back after a long time away. It's not easy. Relax!'

I wasn't naïve. I had expected to have some issues rediscovering the city of my childhood that had, over the years, developed a romantic, sepia-toned hue. I'd never worked in India before and knew I'd have to adjust to a more relaxed and inefficient culture. Yet, I had faith in my inherent *Bombayness,* that indefatigable spirit would see me through.

'Had I known, I'd have never transferred here,' I muttered.

'Who's causing you grief now? Disha asked, tossing the cushions on the floor and beaching herself on the sofa. 'Cook? Driver? I liked him. What's his name? Ashish?'

'Aatish. Bloody idiot. Nearly killed me.'

'Don't exaggerate…'

'I'm not! He nearly drove into a wall the other night. Night blindness…' I shook my head. 'What? What's funny?'

'Sorry, I shouldn't laugh but…'

'I could have died.'

'Rubbish. Bet the chap wasn't driving over ten, given the traffic. Where was this *wall?*'

'Okay, it was while he was parking downstairs. Hardly the point. Why is it so hard to find decent Help? This country is a dump.'

'Calm down.'

'I'm this bloody close to booking a flight.'

'You've been saying that for weeks! Look, obviously there was something that compelled you to come back here. Try to remember that, okay? For what its worth, Ma and I love having you back. Although that shouldn't sway you either way. Whatever works for you.'

I leaned back on the sofa and thought of the relative sanity of the life I'd left behind. I wouldn't admit it to her – hell, I could barely understand it myself. Despite its efficiency and charm, and the fact that I had a good job and a decent set of friends, my life in London had started to feel empty. At some level, I found myself yearning for something I couldn't quite define. And frustrating as Bombay was, having family around came with certain advantages.

'Hello? Are you listening? You coming to Ma's tonight? Biryani.'

'Not in the mood. Tell her to save me some, I'll pop by after my *driver interview,*' I snorted.

'I'll drop some over on my way home. Need you carb-loaded before your big day!' Disha giggled.

'Get out,' I grinned, despite myself. 'Thanks.'

'It's what sisters do. See you later.'

I waved her off and slumped back onto the sofa.

I'd moved to London nearly twenty years ago and for the most part had loved it. As a student at Imperial, I'd enjoyed the camaraderie at halls, the joys of late-night Chinese takeaways, the chaos of printing essays last-minute at the cranky communal printer and the thrill of cheap-booze-infused sex before swapping it for the demands of a post as city Consultant. I got promoted, I fell in love, travelled and bought a flat. A few years later, I fell out of love. Then, the recession hit and London lost a bit of her sparkle. I watched as my friends moved away, spreading themselves like a cloak across the globe. I found myself working more, going out less and the cold began to bother me, in a way it never had before.

I needed sunshine. I considered moving to Dubai and Singapore. Both were enticing enough but despite the lure of no taxes and the promise of well-oiled efficiency, they didn't feel right. But I was desperate for change. So finally, one particularly grim October afternoon, as I watched the rain trickle like a weak stream of piss across my window-pane, I decided I'd had enough. I applied for a transfer to the Bombay office and, within weeks, was packed and on a flight to the city of my childhood.

Getting here had been easy. Settling in was the hard bit.

My confidence started to crumble a week after I moved into my flat, a snazzy penthouse overlooking the Arabian sea. Disha's reaction didn't bode well either.

'This flat is a problem. It reeks of...*expatness.*'

'You can't just make up words.'

'Whatever. You'll be ripped off, you know.'

'By whom?'

'Everyone.' She waved her arms around my kitchen. 'Look at this stuff. And what the hell's this?'

'Vitamix.'

'But you hate soup. Since when do you drink juice?'

'I don't.' I shrugged. 'It's cool.'

She rolled her eyes. 'You're a dollar sign.'

'Nonsense. I speak Hindi.'

'A Hindi-speaking Dollar sign then. Look, let me organise things for you, sort out the Help.'

'My company's got a relocation agent who's going to do all that.'

203

'Trust me, these relocation chaps are useless. Also, you're not used to haggling, let me do it.'

'Relax,' I smiled. 'Have a coffee. This baby makes the best espressos.'

A few weeks of excellent expressos later, my coffee machine, the pride and joy I'd cradled like a newborn in my hand-luggage from Heathrow, emitted a series of sparks and filled the kitchen with the smell of burned rubber.

'Woltage difference, Sir,' muttered the hastily summoned electrician. 'So sad.'

'Shit. Can you…'

'I fikshing, yes! Fikshing many things. Washingmachineirondryerthoasther…everythings!' He ran his fingers over the smoky carcass. 'But, expensiwe. Parts from foreign.'

'How much?'

He scribbled some numbers on the back of his palm. 'I thinking…' he nodded. 'Yes. Two thousand. Ekshactly and approkshimately.'

'What? For that price I could buy a brand new machine here!'

'Ah yes, Sir. Buth I knowing, this machine not *av-lable* in India. No fix, no machine. But okay. Phipteen hundred..

Bugger. 'Okay. But you must…'

'I do best job, Sir! Not needing worrying!' He bundled the machine into a canvas bag. 'You wanting espress service? One day only. Extra phive-hundred rupees, but for you, discount. Three-phiphty only.'

An extra three quid. I knew I was being ripped off, but couldn't be arsed to haggle anymore. 'Fine.'

'I come back phast-phast,' he muttered piously, pinching the skin on his neck between his thumb and forefinger. 'Phipty-percent upfront,' he said, extending his palm.

'What for?'

'Buy parts, Sir.'

I couldn't bring myself to argue, it required too much effort. I thrust the notes into the outstretched bowl of his hand and hurried him out the door.

'I come tomorrow morning itself! God Promise!' he twinkled and scuttled off.

'What do you mean he hasn't shown up?' Disha said the following afternoon when I phoned her in a panic. 'Call him!'

'His phone's off.'

'Do you have the address of his shop?'

'Nope. Only his mobile.'

'Where'd you find this fellow?'

'How does that matter?'

'Answer the bloody question, Rohan.'

'I asked the security chap downstairs to recommend an electrician and he said his brother's neighbor, or maybe its his neighbour's brother, I'm not sure...and before you ask, it was the security fellow's last day at work yesterday so I've no way of contacting him either.'

'Why didn't you just call me?'

'Are you going to help me find this chap or not?'

'How the hell am I supposed to do that? Forget it. I'll send my guy tomorrow. He's good. Reliable.'

'He took my machine.'

'What? Speak clearly. EN-UN-CIATE.'

I closed my eyes in preparation of the inevitable. 'He took. My. Machine.'

No number of trumpets could have drowned out my sister's laughter. 'So you're telling me you paid this *goonda* money to nick your machine? From under your bloody nose! Brilliant!' she snorted.

'You sound like Ma when you do that.'

'Shut up. Don't change the subject.'

'This place is a bloody nightmare.'

'I'm sorry, Rohan, you're the twit here. You wouldn't have got some goon to fix your machine in London would you? Why here?'

'I'd have chucked it in the bin and ordered a new one, same day delivery. But this particular model isn't available in this cesspit...'

'Hardly the point, you know what I mean. You're allowing your nostalgia for this place to override your common sense. That, and the fact that you keep converting to pounds and thinking it's beyond you to haggle. You're not the first, and you wont be the last, but the sooner you wake up...'

'It never used to be like this,' I whined.

'It's *always* been like this. You need to keep your wits about you; a lot of these guys are opportunists. Can't blame them really, given how little they have, but you've got to be careful. Remember Bunty? Ma's cook?'

'Yeah.'

'She chucked him out because he nicked her ring. And remember Patel?'

'Who?'

'The gardener.'

'Oh him! Yeah! Gaurav and I'd play cricket with him and...'

'Yeah, that him. Kept borrowing money from old Mrs. Singh and when she asked him to pay her back, he vanished.'

'Never liked her. Bloody grouch, she used to yell when...'

'Irrelevant. My point is you can't let your familiarity override your common sense. I know this place feels like home, hell, it is, but don't let that lull you into a false sense of security.'

Her words hit me like a fist. She was right. I'd wrapped myself in the warm blanket of familiarity, viewing everyone through the rose-tinted lenses of my childhood.

'Enough of that. Drinks tonight? Willingdon? Anything to help you cope with this latest tragedy.'

It's not funny, it made the...'

'Best espressos, yeah,' she giggled. 'See you at eight.'

Elvis coughed. 'Sir? Now not good time? I come back?'

I rubbed my temples. All I wanted to do was have a coffee, shower and eat breakfast, in no particular order. It had been a busy week with lots of boozy dinners and I hadn't yet recovered from the shock of the brazen abduction of my coffee machine. I was tempted to ask Elvis to return later, but it was far too soon after the goon-masquerading-as-electrician-episode to risk it. And I desperately needed a driver.

The relocation agency was responsible for this mess. They were to arrange a cook and driver, as part of my relocation package. The cook was a surly-arsed disappointment, but at least he showed up. The driver never did. They sent another chap but less than a week later he told me he needed a month off for his upcoming wedding and honeymoon. Needless to say, I told him to buzz off. The next guy proved incapable of showing up to work on time. Finally, they sent me the night-blind Aatish, and I'd had enough. I told the relocation agency to shove it, and that I'd drive myself to work. And I did, for a week. The morning traffic was awful as was the near-futility of finding a parking spot. I tried Uber which was as reliable as the District Line on a rainy London morning. Which left me no choice but Bombay's iconic black-and-yellow-taxicabs. I'd loved them as a boy, with their garish interiors, and had made a point of taking a cab every time I visited the city on holiday from London.

In what can only be described as perversion masquerading as nostalgia, I jumped into a cab to go to work one morning. The rattling nearly gave me a hernia, preferable though to spending all day with a dubious oily stain on my trousers that ran from my crotch to my knee. No one said anything but I noticed a few well-meaning strips of Imodium in my desk drawer the following day. *Enough is enough,* I muttered, tossing the pills in the bin. I spent the rest of the morning calling my friends, asking them if they could recommend a driver.

'I know a guy,' offered Gaurav. 'Worked for a friend of my Dad. I'll send him over to you. Sunday morning at nine?'

'Yes!' I breathed with relief. 'Thanks, man.'

The driver tapped his foot. 'Sir?'

'Sorry, yes. What's your name again?'

'Elvis, Sir.'

'Okay, Elvis.' I tossed the keys over to him. 'Let's see how you drive.'

'But no breakfast, Sir? Brother making. Omelette, fry-egg, post-egg…'

'Post-egg?'

'Very good he makes! You try! Break egg in hot water and…'

208

I groaned. 'No, poached eggs, thank you. Let's go.'

The drive was uncontroversial. True to his ilk, he demonstrated a healthy disrespect for basic traffic rules but apart from that minor detail, he seemed competent.

'Okay, Elvis. Job's yours. You need to report for duty at 7.30 every morning. Sunday's are off.'

'Yessir.'

'Now salary,' I began.

'What you tinking is best, Sir.'

Shit. More bloody haggling. Just the thought made my head throb. Also, I'd no idea where to begin. I should've asked Disha, or Gaurav.

'Why don't you…'

'How I can, Sir? You say.'

'Fine. Twenty thousand a month.'

Elvis looked at me as though I'd just confessed to crucifying his first-born.

'Elvis?'

'How I can, Sir? Old Boss paying twenty-two thousand, plus Diwali plus Chrissmas bonus plus overtimes! Also you wanting me coming earlys and leaving lates. You check here, see,' he continued, pulling out his phone and punching the keypad. 'You speak to Baby, here.' He thrust the phone into my palm.

'Baby?'

'Daughter of Old-Boss. Anhaita-baby.'

Ah yes. Another Indian idiosyncrasy. An employer's offspring was always Baby or Baba, irrespective of their age. It wouldn't surprise me if Anhaita were a hip-replacement toting geriatric herself.

'I'm not talking to this *Baby*,' I handed him the phone and pressed my temples. This haggling thing was a nuisance. 'Okay, Elvis, twenty-two. No more.'

'Plus overtimes.'

'Fine,' I sighed, desperate for my hell to end.

'Thank you, Sir!' he beamed, pumping my hand. 'You will not regretting, I best…'

'Yeah, Elvis. Drive to Starbucks, please. Now.'

Disha stood up, frowning, as I pushed the door open. 'You're late.'

'Sorry.' I kissed my sister's cheek. 'Met the boys for a beer and lost track of time.'

'You're always boozing these days.'

'Jeez, come on…'

'Relax, I'm joking. What're we drinking?'

'We're celebrating tonight. Champagne!'

'*Arre vah!* New coffee machine?'

'No need to be snarky,' I scowled. 'Still stings you know?'

'Sorry,' she grinned, reaching for my fags. 'What, then?'

'Hired a driver! Starts tomorrow. Seems okay. Super-enthusiastic, but whatever. Kept trying to shove his brother down my throat though. Bloody pest.'

She narrowed her eyes. 'I hope you were firm with him and said no. It's the latest thing. Invariably the chap has a job already so tries to palm it off on his friend.'

'Stop. I've a good feeling about this one. His name's Elvis.'

'Elvis! Excellent. Sounds like an improvement on the murderous Aatish already. Cheers!' She clinked her flute with mine. 'What're you paying him?'

'Twenty, plus overtime.' The lie slid smooth off my tongue, like honey.

'TWENTY THOU?'

'Ssh! Can you not shout? You're just like Ma…'

'Shut up. Are you mad? Nineteen would've been plenty! Ma pays Thakor eighteen-and-a-half, you know?'

'And Thakor's half-deaf and doesn't know his gear from his elbow,' I retorted, trying to ignore the sinking feeling in my stomach.

'Forget it. How's your cook?'

'Fine,' I snapped.

'So why is Ma sending you food this week then?'

'He quit.'

'Obviously. Why?'

'Refused to cut veggies and do the washing up. Said his job was *cooking only*, and that I should hire someone to do the rest. Said that he had a helper in his previous job and couldn't work without one. Wants a goddamned *sous-chef* and…what?'

'Nothing.' The corners of her mouth twitched.

'Anyway, he said he'd *consider* cutting the veg. for an extra grand a month and…what's funny?'

'This! Come on, Rohan! You pay a guy money to steal your coffee machine. Your driver's called Elvis and your cook's quite the diva,' she said, shaking with laughter.

'I've bloody had it with this dump.'

'It's not so bad. Think of it as the price you pay for this,' she waved her arms. 'Early February and we're sitting outside, nice breeze…'

'Hmph.'

'How's work?' Disha tactfully changed the subject.

I slipped off my loafers and ran my feet over the grass. 'I'm enjoying it.'

'Really?'

I nodded. 'Things take longer, sure, which is annoying. But its more relaxed. Social too. Nitin's invited me for dinner with his family on the weekend.'

'Family dinner with the Boss,' she grinned. 'All these meals out, no wonder you're getting fat.'

I ignored her. 'You know, six years I worked for Rupert, and nothing. Sure, the odd pint here and there but that was it. Nothing personal.'

'I thought he liked you?'

'I'm sure he does. Gave me a glowing recommendation, actually. Probably just a cultural thing.'

'See? It's not all bad here. Stop sulking and give it time.'

'I don't sulk, I just bloody…'

'Whatever.' She tapped her glass. 'Get some more champagne.'

I swore under my breath and ordered another bottle.

My heart soared at the buzz of the doorbell the following morning. *Great, he's punctual,* I beamed, opening the door.

'Where's Elvis?'

'Bad news, Sir. Mother she very sick. Elvis gone visit Mother in village,' the brother mumbled in an entirely unconvincing monotone.

I glared at him. 'Why didn't he call?'

'What to saying? He go in hurry. But he coming back, Jejuz-promise. Now I here. I make breakfast?'

'No! I have a meeting…Shit! I need to leave.' Disha's warning from the previous night rang in my ears, but now wasn't the time. 'Here,' I tossed him the keys.

He whistled tunelessly in the lift in an attempt to break the crust of uneasy silence that had settled between us. In the lobby, he turned to me. 'Wait here, Sir. I bring car.'

I nodded and began scrolling through my phone. A drinks invite for Thursday night, a text from Gaurav wanting to know if I was up for a round of golf on Saturday morning, and an e-mail from a cousin in Goa, asking me to visit her over a weekend the following month. Eighteen years I'd been gone, but it hardly mattered. It was like I'd never left. And that's when it hit me. It was this, an all-pervading sense of inclusion that I'd missed for most of the time I'd been away. Despite the chaos and the confusion that had characterised the past few weeks, I couldn't deny the blanket of belonging that had wrapped itself around me, one that I knew I'd struggle to find elsewhere.

'It's not all bad, Disha's right,' I muttered, turning my gaze to a trio of fat parakeets balanced incongruously on a telephone wire, their noisy twitter drowning out the crash of the waves in the distance. I thought of the grey London mornings I'd left behind. Of the cold rain and the emptiness that had clung to me like a shadow; a feeling, I now realised, I hadn't felt in weeks. It had all been replaced by a warm sense of security.

My mobile buzzed. Disha.

'Elvis rock up yet?' she chuckled.

I groaned. 'Don't ask. Anyway, I'm glad you called. Di, I'm going to rent out my flat...'

She gasped.

'Now calm down,' I began hastily. 'Nothing long term, six months tops, but I think I'm ready to give this place...' I looked up to see the brother running toward me. 'Di, I'll call you back.'

'Sir! I try start car but...'

'But?'

'Clutch, Sir!' he panted. 'The clutch!'

'Huh?'

'In car! No clutch! How to change gear?'

'GODDAMN IT!' I exploded. 'Are you a driver or what? Bloody cheats, all of you!' I snatched the keys off him. 'You're FIRED! And you tell your brother, Elvis, not to show his face here. In fact,' I continued, indignant, 'I'm going to instruct security to stop either of you from ever entering the building again.' I nodded with righteous indignation. 'Hey, Watchman?' I called.

The pot-bellied guard ambled over, a look of detached amusement on his face. 'Problem, Sir?'

'Yes! You are not to allow driver Elvis or this man, his brother… you, what's your name?'

'Name, Sir?' stuttered the brother. 'Myself, Englebert.'

I stared at him for a moment before reaching for my mobile.

'Disha?' I began. 'You won't believe it, but…'

And then, much to my sister's delight, not to mention the confusion of the gormless faces in front of me, I threw my head back and laughed.

London could wait. It was time for some fun.

DINNER PARTY IN THE HOME COUNTIES

Reshma Ruia

Being peripheral
I can't offer opinions on climate change
Oil prices or the Brexit crisis
I could be an exotic butterfly
Or a rare breed of monkey
Well-meaning pale white hands freckled brown
Finger cautiously the paisley filigree of my
Mysore silk shawl
Their voices turn bold
Their eyes throw hooks
'Is female infanticide still common?'
'Are you going for an arranged marriage?'
'How long before you go back?'
The questions fly like arrows thick and fast
Wounding me until my skin is a battleground
How gratified they look
It's a personal triumph

When I don't drop my cutlery or my vowels
Ethnic? I don't know what that word means
I become a colour when I enter certain rooms
But what I feel think or eat
I refuse to accept as marginal
I choose not to talk of sacred cows
Or Sadhus floating in a Yogic trance
I have as much right as anyone else
To claim this slice of sky as my own
To plant my flag and sow my seed
I will not be pushed to the edges of a map
My face pinned to a rogue's gallery
Labelled minority alternative arts

THE WHOLE KAHANI

Reshma Ruia is the co-founder of The Whole Kahani. Her first novel, *Something Black in the Lentil Soup*, was described in the Sunday Times as 'a gem of straight-faced comedy.' Her second novel, *A Mouthful of Silence*, was shortlisted for the 2014 SI Leeds Literary Prize.Her short stories and poems have appeared in various International anthologies and magazines and also commissioned for Radio 4. She has a PhD and Masters with Distinction in Creative Writing and post graduate and undergraduate degrees from the London School of Economics. Born in India, but brought up in Italy, her narrative portrays the inherent tensions and preoccupations of those who possess multiple senses of belonging. @RESHMARUIA

Kavita A. Jindal is the co-founder of The Whole Kahani. Her poetry collection *Raincheck Renewed* was published to critical acclaim by Chameleon Press and the manuscript for her debut novel won the Brighthorse Novel Prize 2018 and was also shortlisted for the 2018 Impress Prize. Her stories, poems and essays have appeared in anthologies and literary journals in the UK and around the world and been broadcast on BBC Radio 4, Zee TV and European radio stations. She won the *Foyles/Vintage 'Haruki Murakami' Prize* in 2012 and received the *Word Masala Award for Excellence in Poetry* in 2016. Kavita serves as Senior Editor at Asia Literary Review. www.kavitajindal.com @writerkavita

Photo by
Kashif Haque

Mona Dash writes fiction and poetry. Her work includes a novel, *Untamed Heart* (Tara India Research Press, 2016), and two collections of poetry *Dawn-Drops* (Writer's Workshop, 2001) and *A Certain Way.* (Skylark Publications 2017). She has a Masters in Creative Writing with distinction from the London Metropolitan University. She was awarded the Poet of Excellence award in the House of Lords in 2016. Her short stories have been listed in various competitions, notably, she won the Asian Writer 2018 compettion, and her short story collection *Let us look elsewhere* was shortlisted for the 2018 SI Leeds Literary prize. Her memoir, *A Roll of The Dice: a story of love, loss and genetics* will be published by Linen Press in 2019. Mona leads a double life: she is a Telecoms Engineer with a MBA and works full time for a global technology organisation. Originally from India, she lives in London.

Photo by
Jags Parbha

Radhika Kapur has won awards for her work as a creative director in advertising at Cannes, One Show, Asia Pacific Adfest and Clio. She is a short fiction and screenwriter. Her writing has appeared in literary journals like the Feminist Review, Poem International and the anthology *Love Across a Broken Map*. She won third place in the Euroscript Screenwriting Competition (2015) was longlisted for the BBC Script Room 12 (Drama – 2017) and the London Short Story Prize (2016). She has recently completed an MA in Screenwriting from Birkbeck College, University of London.

CG Menon is the author of *Subjunctive Moods*, published by Dahlia Publishing. She's won or been placed in a number of competitions, including the Fish, Bridport, Bare Fiction and Short Fiction Journal awards. Her work has been broadcast on radio, and she's been a judge for several international short fiction competitions. She has a PhD in pure mathematics and is studying for a creative writing MA at City University. She's currently working on her first novel, set in 1980s Malaysia.

Shibani Lal was born in Bombay and moved to the UK in 2000. She was runner-up in the Asian writer prize and was longlisted for the Bristol prize and Cambridge short-story prize. Shibani holds an MA from Edinburgh, an MPhil from Cambridge and has worked in the City for over a decade. She's also had brief stints in Singapore and Paris where she trained as a pastry chef and is a keen open-water swimmer: she's swum from the BVI to the USVI and recently swam from Asia to Europe, across the Bosphorous. Shibani splits her time between London and Bombay and is currently working on a novel.

Deblina Chakrabarty is a freelance writer and a Bombayite who relocated to London 7 years ago. Since 2005 she's written for various publications in India including Times of India, DNA, Man's World, and various other dailies as well as magazines. She's primarily interested in the chasm between genders, cultures, cities and lovers that form open terrain for the curious examinations of her pen (well, keyboard). By day she flirts on the fringes of storytelling, working for international distribution at a major Hollywood studio.

Nadia Kabir Barb is a writer and journalist. She is the author of the short story collection, *Truth or Dare*. Her work has been published in international literary journals and anthologies such as, Wasafiri, The Missing Slate, Open Road Review, Six Seasons Review, Bengal Lights, Eclectic Mix Volume 5 and was the winner of the Audio Arcadia short story competition. She holds an MSc from The London School of Economics and The London School of Hygiene and Tropical Medicine and has worked in the health and development sector in both Bangladesh and the UK. She was a long standing columnist for The Daily Star Bangladesh.

Preti Taneja was born in England to Indian parents. She has worked with youth charities and with refugees, and in conflict and post-conflict zones on minority and cultural rights. She teaches writing in prisons and universities. She is the co-founder of the advocacy collective ERA Films and of Visual Verse, an online anthology of art and words. *We That Are Young*, her debut novel was first published in the UK by Galley Beggar Press, in India by Penguin Random House and in North America by A.A Knopf. It was a *Sunday Times*, *Guardian*, *Spectator* and The Hindu Book of the Year, and has been shortlisted for awards including the Jan Michalski Prize, the Shakti Bhatt First Book Prize and the Books Are My Bag Reader's Choice Awards. Is the winner of the Desmond Elliot Prize 2018 for the best debut novel of the year.

9 781999 604660